CAPTIVE VOW

WILLOW FOX

Captive Vow

Mafia Marriages Book Two

Willow Fox

Published by Slow Burn Publishing

Cover design by MiblArt

V2

© 2021

1

PAIGE

I ought to walk out before I end up murdered.

Everything feels off.

The smell of stale cigarette smoke lingers in the air and burns my nostrils. The floral wallpaper is a dirty old yellow.

The hairs on my arm stand on end.

I should turn around.

Run.

But I need a job and the wooden sign hanging outside, squeaking in the wind with the words *Nanny Agency, Inc.,* caught my interest.

"Hello?" I call down an empty hallway.

I step farther into the single-story brick building. The place looks new from the outside, but the appearance inside tells another story.

A rough Italian accent, male, catches me off guard as he comes up from a back stairwell.

Abruptly, he shuts the door behind himself.

"Can I help you?" he asks. He glances at me thoroughly, over, up, and down.

Is he ogling me?

Gross!

He's not the least bit attractive, with his bushy eyebrows and a thick, raised red scar across his cheek and arms. It looks like Hook left his mark after he fought with a crocodile.

While I realize that I'm not dressed in a suit or blazer, I have on a nice pair of jeans and a blouse. I wasn't planning on stopping in for an interview, just an application.

"I saw your sign when I was driving by," I say.

He steps closer and reaches for the speaker, turning the radio louder, though I don't have the slightest idea as to why.

There are only the two of us in the building.

It's a rather rude gesture, and I have half a mind to run before I end up chopped up in his cellar, but I also need a job. And I'm good with kids.

Aside from Mr. Ogling Scar Face, there's no one else who I notice in the office.

I start again, deciding maybe I need to be more direct in my approach. "I'm Paige Stone. I have previous experience as a preschool director and owner of a preschool facility in Spring Valley. I'd like to find out if you have any nanny openings available."

"We have an opening that we haven't been able to fill yet," the gentleman says. He glances me up and down again.

Is it something about my appearance? I glance down to make sure there isn't a stain on my shirt or a hole in my jeans that I missed.

"You're a little older than our usual girls who come in."

"I don't know what kind of nanny operation you're running here, but I have plenty of experience, and as far as I'm concerned, if you're discriminating based on age or body type, I'll contact an attorney."

His brow tightens.

"That isn't necessary," he seethes. His hands clench into fists.

My threat seems to have intimidated him.

Good!

I reach for a business card on the nearby desk, prepared to file a complaint if he doesn't at least give me an application to fill out.

"Are you Vance DeLuca?" I ask, reading the name on the card.

"I am," he says.

There's no hint of a smile, and the whole place wreaks of trouble, but I'm not intending to nanny for him or his family. He's just the middleman, the broker, and I need a job.

2

PAIGE

The doorbell jingles as I step foot inside the small café. I'm early for my job interview and don't want to show up before my appointment.

Thankfully, I only had to wait a day for the interview.

Sleeping in my car sucks.

I grab an overpriced coffee and then a seat at a table, keeping an eye on the time.

My focus is primarily on my phone. The coffee shop at two in the afternoon is pretty quiet, except for the hiss and whirl of the machines as the barista prepares a coffee for another customer.

I glance up briefly from my phone and offer a weak smile.

I grew up in Breckenridge, but it feels like a lifetime ago. The last time I was here, I helped pack up Mom's house and had her move in with me. Now that she's gone, coming home just feels right.

Maybe it's because the town holds fond memories.

Who says you can't go home again?

At least, I want to believe that to be the case.

Another glance at my phone and the position that the nanny agency suggested might be a good fit.

Businessman seeks full-time nanny to special needs girl. Includes room & board along with a modest stipend.

The gentleman at the counter grabs his drink and pauses, giving me the once over. "Paige?"

He's tall, handsome, and has a plethora of ink that covers his skin. He's easy on the eyes, and my gaze falls quickly to the wedding band that he's wearing.

Damn.

"Yes?" I don't recognize him.

But he knows me.

"Wow, you don't remember me. Do you?" he asks.

I smile sheepishly and tuck an errant strand of hair behind my ear. I doubt he was covered in ink the last time I saw him.

His grin is wide and bright. He looks genuinely happy.

That's how I want to feel. I hope living here, moving here, can bring me that same type of joy.

"Jaxson Monroe," he says and holds out his hand.

I smile and nod, pretending to recognize him. "Right."

I could never be an actress. In all honesty, I have no clue who he is, but he's drop-dead gorgeous. Like he just walked right off the cover of a romance book.

"You don't remember me," he says.

Well, he knows who I am. My name isn't that common. "I guess I haven't changed that much," I say with a laugh. "I'm betting you didn't have those tattoos the last time we saw each other."

Jaxson smiles warmly and laughs. He shakes his head. "I'd say not. High school was the last time we saw each other, but I'd say we went to junior high and elementary school together. I won't take any offense. Promise." He gives a scout's honor gesture.

He doesn't quite look like a boy scout, but I smile politely. I've plastered a grin on my face to not seem so out of sorts.

He doesn't grasp I'm uncomfortable, or maybe he's just one of those super friendly and outgoing guys who doesn't realize that other people aren't great at making conversation.

He's lucky.

I'm not.

"Are you visiting family?" Jaxson asks.

My lips tighten for a brief second. "No. I decided to move back here for a job." I glance at my watch. "I have an interview to get to."

I stand and take the remnants of my coffee with me, dropping it into the trash.

"Good luck."

"Thank you. It was nice seeing you again, Jaxson," I say over my shoulder.

———

The café shop was bright, sunny, and felt friendly, probably because I ran into Jaxson.

I pull up outside the address for my interview. It's a dive bar.

"Seriously?"

What kind of businessman interviews for a nanny at a bar? I need the job, and being pretentious isn't going to help me land the gig.

I'm only about five minutes early. I turn my phone on silent, grab my resume from the front seat and step out of my sedan.

I slam the car door and head inside wearing an A-line skirt, blouse, a short-sleeved sweater, and high heels.

Dress for the job you want.

What does a nanny wear, exactly?

I'm no Mary Poppins. And let's face it, I need the job more than she ever did.

If I don't get the job, I'll be sleeping in my car indefinitely.

Every cent was spent on hospital bills, the funeral, and taking care of my mother before her passing.

The door is heavy and squeaks on its hinges as I yank it open.

It takes a moment for my eyes to adjust to the dimness, and I glance around, looking for a gentleman in a business suit.

There aren't too many people in the bar. Two men are playing pool in leather jackets. They probably belong in a motorcycle club.

The bartender nods toward the back of the bar.

There's a booth in the corner. The table has a placard marked *reserved*.

I saunter up to the gentleman seated in the booth. The hairs on my arms stand on end. Something feels not quite right, but I push all my fears and anxiety aside.

It's probably me being nervous.

"Hi, I'm Paige Stone," I say and hold out my hand to introduce myself.

"Moreno Ricci," he introduces. "Please, have a seat."

The booth is curved, and I do my best to sit as far from him as possible. This isn't a date. I don't want it to feel cozy.

Why didn't he pick a table or a booth where we were seated across from one another? Hell, why didn't he choose another place to meet?

He's dressed sharply, in a suit, his white shirt crisp, his tie without a single flaw. "Tell me about yourself, Paige."

His question almost comes off as sounding a little too personal, like a date. But I know I'm reading into it. This is a job interview.

He will be my boss if I'm hired.

"Yes, of course." I slide over a copy of my resume. I also keep a second copy for myself to glance down at every so often. It helps me focus on what I want to say and keeps me from leaving out something important.

"I owned and operated a preschool in Spring Valley until late last fall when a buyer offered to purchase the establishment."

I don't want to elaborate on why I sold the business.

Not unless he asks.

His eyes tighten and he gives a weak nod. "Owning a preschool isn't the same as working with children."

"I have a degree in early education, and I spent a decade teaching preschool-aged children and writing a curriculum that other teachers used for my private preschool. You mentioned in your listing that your daughter is special needs. I have lots of experience working with a variety of children with unique requirements."

"That's all well and good," Moreno says, "however, you need to understand that since this job includes room and board, you may see things that I can't have you asking questions about or speaking of to anyone."

"I don't know anyone here," I say. Well, that's not true. I almost don't know anyone. I ran into Jaxson earlier this morning, but he hardly counts. It's not like we're friends and sharing secrets. I don't know where he lives or his phone number. He's also married, from what I could tell, the ring a dead giveaway.

I haven't exactly kept in touch with any of my childhood friends. Most of them moved away, I assume.

Moreno tightens his lips. "Secrecy is expected and seen as highly regarded above all else."

He retrieves a briefcase and removes a series of papers and a pen.

"If you are interested, my employer and I require that you sign these papers to assure us that you understand your responsibilities and will keep everything you witness or overhear confidential."

"That's it. I sign the papers and the job is mine?" I ask.

I haven't even met the little girl I'm supposed to be a nanny for yet, but I can't imagine a four-year-old is that much of a terror. Even if she is, I need this job, and Moreno seems to need me.

"You will need to meet with my daughter, Nova, but that cannot happen until after you've signed the papers," Moreno says.

I can't imagine he brought Nova with him. "Do you own this place?" I ask, glancing around the bar. I can't fathom why else he suggested that we meet here.

"My boss owns the place," Moreno says and clears his throat.

Does he notice my discomfort?

"I appreciate the discretion that I'm offered here," he says.

"I see."

"Do you?" Moreno asks.

No, not really. I reach for the pages of documentation that he has requested I review and sign. "The agency had me already fill out a bunch of paperwork," I say.

"Yes, I'm sure they did, but we require anyone coming into our home to understand and abide by our rules. Besides, the contract for hire is with us. We pay the agency for bringing you to us."

My attention returns to the packet of documents that he wants me to sign. There's an entire page on discretion, secrecy, and that I am to always follow his instructions.

He's got a bit of a complex. That's for sure.

But this job is better than sleeping in my car. And while I could apply at the coffee shop where I stopped this morning, I doubt it would pay enough for me to rent an apartment locally.

The fact that I'm offered room and board makes it worthwhile.

I scribble my name on the line and initial the individual pages he taps one at a time.

I skim over the specifics of the contract. It's ninety-fricking pages. I would be here all day if I read every line, but I get the gist. Don't disclose anything I witness, overhear, or find.

Satisfied with my signature, he places the pages back into his briefcase and slides out of the booth. "If you'd like to follow me, I can lead you to the property."

I slip out of the booth and stand, smoothing down my skirt.

Moreno takes long, quick strides, and I practically have to run in my high heels to catch up with him.

He throws open the heavy wooden door, and the bright afternoon light forces me to squint.

"Where's your vehicle?"

I point to the two-door sedan. It's not much, but I haven't needed anything extravagant.

He snorts under his breath. "That's not going to get you up and around the mountain in winter. I'll go slow since I'm betting you don't have all-wheel drive on that thing."

"Do you want to give me the address and I can put it into my phone?"

"GPS is spotty out here," Moreno says. "Especially when we head farther off the beaten path."

"Oh, okay." I climb into my car and follow behind Moreno in his shiny black SUV. It looks brand new—even the wheels sparkle.

I'm driving a stick shift, and I downshift as I follow him up the mountain and then off the main road. We drive for a while with the forest at both sides, and then to the left is a clearing, open fields and haystacks abound.

It's beautiful.

Moreno turns on his signal, and we head down a narrow driveway. Trees canopy above the road, making it feel like a bridge as we near the property.

Wrought-iron gates tower above and stretch on as far as I can see. We pull to a halt, and there's a guard tower with a man inside the booth.

The forest is in the distance, but a clearing stretches on for two properties, with one giant log cabin. It's remote but beautiful. The cabin is freshly stained, the wood bright with the sun shining against it, and huge. It very well could be described as a mansion, but from the outside, it's rustic, not the least bit frilly.

What exactly does Moreno do for a living?

The gates part and I drive through slowly behind Moreno, giving the guard a brief nod of thanks as I enter the premises.

Private security?

I hit the jackpot getting room and board at a place like this.

It beats sleeping in my car.

Who does Moreno work for?

The C.I.A.?

3

MORENO

I park the SUV in front of the house and wait for Paige to park behind me.

"Ready?" It's not really a question. I escort her inside, the front door locked, and the security system armed. I disarm it upon entering. There's also a guard on duty at the main entrance to the foyer.

Leone isn't usually on duty at the front entrance. Most of the time, we don't require a guard to watch the door since we have a guard gate at the main entrance.

But today is different.

Bringing a stranger into the compound requires extra precautions. Leone has been assigned to watch over the new nanny when she's unaccompanied by Don Ricci or me.

Paige is quiet and follows with soft footsteps. Her heels click against the wooden floorboards as she follows me through the foyer and around the hallway to the playroom downstairs.

"You decided to wear that to an interview for a nanny position?" I glance at Paige. By the time we're done, she's likely to have ruined her nice clothes.

Her brow furrows and she fixes her jacket and skirt.

I undoubtedly insulted her, but she has worked with kids before. She owned a preschool. Paige should have expected to wear something a bit more practical.

"You have a lovely home." She ignores my remark.

"Thank you." I don't correct her to tell her it's not my home. Dante has afforded me the privilege of living under his roof. It is an honor, and because he has eight bedrooms, there's no issue regarding space.

Besides, Luca and Nova are practically inseparable, minus the time that Luca is in kindergarten.

I head into the playroom and discover Luca painting on the canvas and Nova enjoying a tea party with her stuffed animals.

Dante's attention is on his phone, his back to the wall, leaning against it. "Oh good, you're here with the new nanny." He barely glances up. "Nikki had a doctor's appointment. I need to check on a shipment coming in. Do you have this?"

"Yes, boss."

Dante jets out of the playroom.

It's always business. I'm honestly shocked he didn't have Leone or Rhys watch Nova and Luca, although the last time Rhys was asked to sit in, the walls were covered in permanent marker.

"Hi, Moreno," Luca says. His back is to me as he continues to paint a picture of our home.

I clear my throat. "Nova, we have a visitor."

She glances up from her tea party and bats her bright blue eyes. She has her mother's baby blues and strawberry-blonde hair. Some days I wonder if she's even mine, but I know she is. Serene had only been with one man, ever.

"Nova, come over here."

She hesitates, like always.

"Nova," I say again. I am trying to remain calm. I need this to work with the new nanny. I can't keep an eye on Nova and continue my role as Dante's second in command.

Being an underboss to the don of the family is no easy task. It's not a nine-to-five job. Whatever Dante needs, I do for him.

Wordlessly, Nova pushes back the chair. It squeaks against the floorboards before it topples over behind her.

She may be mute, but her actions are nothing of the sort.

Nova stands, but she doesn't listen. She never listens to me.

With a heavy sigh, I stalk over and grab Nova's arm, bringing her toward Paige.

"Paige, this is my daughter, Nova."

"Hi, Nova," Paige says, and immediately she bends down to Nova's level. "I like your stuffed animal collection."

Nova gnaws on her bottom lip and glances over her shoulder at her stuffed animals.

"Would it be okay for you to show me your friends?" Paige asks my daughter.

Nova glances from the nanny to me.

"Go ahead, you can show her your toys," I say.

Folding my arms across my chest, I watch their interaction.

Paige is soft spoken with Nova and smiles warmly. She's trying to ease my daughter's fears. I get that.

But it's not going to work.

Nova requires a firm hand and a strong, authoritative figure. Coddling her is the last thing to help the situation. She doesn't listen, her mind constantly in a state of daydreaming and wandering.

"Which friend is your favorite?" Paige asks.

Nova doesn't answer.

"She can't answer you," I remind Paige.

Her eyes tighten, and she smiles warmly at Nova. "I'll be right back."

Nova's eyes are wide, and she drops to the floor to sit with her stuffed animals, her legs folded beneath her.

"May I have a word with you, alone?" Paige asks.

There's a fire behind her gaze.

She's going to bring trouble.

4

PAIGE

"May I have a word with you alone, sir?" I ask.

"Of course. Why don't we step out into the hallway?" Moreno leads me out of the playroom, but we're still in view of Luca and Nova.

His attention appears to be on them more than it is on me.

"If you're hiring me to care for your daughter, then I expect you to listen to my expertise as a caregiver," I say. I know I'm toeing the line. His stupid contract pointed out that he was in charge, and sure, he's the boss, I get that, but I'm not okay with the way he handles his daughter.

I rattle on before he can interrupt me or toss me out the front door.

"You cannot talk to your child in such a manner. Yes, she may not speak, but she can still communicate, and you should be encouraging it in any form."

"Excuse me?" Moreno scoffs. "You're telling me how to raise my daughter?" He steps closer, coming into my personal space.

He forces me to take a step back. His attention is no longer on the children in the room, but entirely on me.

The heat of his stare sends a shiver down my spine.

"You think you know what's best for Nova?" Moreno asks. "Because I can assure you that whatever you think you know, you're mistaken."

His nostrils flare, and I open my mouth but quickly shut it when Luca bursts out screaming at the top of his lungs.

Moreno tears into the playroom and pulls the gun from his holster on his hip.

I didn't even know he had a gun on him. "You're scaring him!" I scold Moreno and rush past him to check on Luca.

Nova's eyes are wide and filled with terror, but she's unmoving, and it seems the only danger is Moreno.

"Mommy!" Luca screams even louder than before. "I want mommy!"

I turn on my heel and point at Moreno. "You need to put that away and step out of here." I gesture toward his gun.

I don't like weapons. I never have. Being around them scares me, but it definitely seems like Luca wins the fear award right now.

Why the hell did Moreno draw his gun? What did he possibly think could have happened that required a weapon in the playroom?

The house is heavily guarded, with gates, guards, and a security system. It is a little overkill.

Moreno heads out of the playroom, and I'm back down on my hands and knees at Luca's level.

"Hey, Luca, I'm Paige," I say, trying to calm him down. "Do you want to show me your painting?" I don't know what originally scared him, but bringing that up now seems a terrible idea.

Nova stands and joins Luca and me beside the canvas.

Luca sniffles and wipes his face with his paint-stained hands, leaving a streak of blue across his cheek.

"I was painting my house," he says. His eyes are red and splotchy, but the tears have slowed.

I smile, genuinely pleased with his painting. "You did a fantastic job," I say.

Nova glances up at me. A faint smile tugs at the corners of her lips. Almost like she's trying not to smile. "Do you like to paint too?" I ask her.

She shrugs her shoulders, not giving me a clear answer.

I'll bet she does like to paint.

"Sorry I'm late." A woman wearing a bright yellow sundress steers into the playroom. "Luca, were you good for the new nanny?" the woman asks as she saunters right over to the little boy. "I'm Nikki," she introduces.

"Hi, I'm Paige," I say and hold out my hand to introduce myself properly. She seems warm, friendly, and completely out of place after meeting Moreno and Dante. "You must be Luca's mom," I guess.

Nikki smiles and nods. "That I am. Are you ready to hit the trails, Luca? Sorry, you got stuck watching this little tiger. I promise it won't be a regular occurrence."

"It was no problem at all," I say. I don't elaborate that I haven't even been here an hour, and Dante had been watching him before I showed up.

"Let me know if you need anything, have any questions, or whatever," Nikki says. "I've got a pretty packed schedule, but I'm happy to help when I have a free minute."

"Thanks."

Nikki escorts Luca out of the playroom. "Come on, Luca. Let's get you washed up. You have paint on your cheek and in your hair. Then we'll go hiking on the trails."

"Okay, Mama." He latches onto her hand and follows her out of the playroom.

It's just Nova and me. I smile warmly and point at her tea party. "Can I play with you and your friends?"

My cell phone buzzes, and I pull it out of my purse to glance at the text message. It's from Moreno.

I glance back at the empty doorframe. He's nowhere in sight. Why didn't he just come talk to me instead of texting me?

The job is yours. Don't screw this up. Nova is counting on you. We both are.

5

MORENO

"The new nanny seems—cute," Dante says, giving me a smirk.

"I didn't notice." It's a lie. How could I not notice her lovely long legs under that skirt?

Dante laughs under his breath. "Of course, you didn't. So, you hired her, I take it."

I rub my forehead. Her experience on paper was excellent, but I wasn't pleased with how she spoke to me. If I said a word about it to Dante, he'd tell me to fire her ass.

"I can't keep interviewing nannies," I say.

"This is your second nanny and first interview since Nova was born."

Dante doesn't beat around the bush.

"Right," I say. "I'm not used to letting outsiders into our home, our lives." I head to the kitchen for a cup of coffee, and Dante follows on my heel. "How's the shipment?" He was dealing with business when I came in this afternoon with Paige.

"Late, but nothing I can't handle. It turns out the truck broke down and was out of cell phone range. You know how the open roads can be," Dante says. "Everything is back on schedule."

"Good." It was one less thing that I'd have to deal with tonight or tomorrow. Dante had done me a favor by handling the shipment. That was my responsibility, and I'd been dealing with hiring a new nanny for Nova.

"You seem different, quiet." Dante is always one step ahead. That used to be me. Ever since the attack on the compound, I've been distracted.

"You know how it is," I excuse and grab the coffee, pouring a cup for myself. I take a sip from the mug. I need the extra dose of caffeine today. I need to be on my toes, especially with Paige under our roof.

Dante's lips are tight. "I can set you up with a place of your own, private security, get Nova and you out from under my roof," he says.

"No." As tempting as the offer is, I can't do that. I wouldn't feel safe without the same level of private security that Dante has for his family. "I'll never be home. We both know that's not ideal with Nova." I didn't hire Paige to raise my daughter, just look after her while I'm distracted with work.

"Have you given the new nanny a private tour of her accommodations and Nova's bedroom?" Dante asks.

I haven't. I bolted out after making a fool of myself in front of the kids. How could I not fear the worst when I heard Luca's terrified scream? Of course, once he saw my gun, the waterworks started, and the hysterical cries grew even louder.

Some days I don't feel cut out to be a father. Serene had been the one who wanted to be a mother. And she'd left me alone with Nova.

Dante was right.

"Not yet. She's with Luca and Nova in the playroom," I say.

I did need to show Paige around. A part of me was avoiding her.

Why was that?

"Nikki just took Luca to go hiking."

"I can't believe you let them go alone." How can he be so careless after the recent attack?

"They're not leaving the property, and one of the guards is with them at all times. They're never alone," Dante says. "I wouldn't have it." He grabs a glass from the counter and then the whiskey in the liquor cabinet and pours a glass for himself. "I'd offer you a drink, but—"

"Yeah, no thanks." I don't drink. My father was an alcoholic, and so I've always been careful to avoid the stuff. I don't want to become my old man.

Dante swirls the amber liquid before swallowing it in one gulp. He pours a second glass for himself. "The nanny you hired, she's cute."

"Don't," I warn him. Why was I feeling overprotective of Paige?

He snickers. "I wasn't suggesting for me. It's been a year, Moreno. Your wife is gone. You deserve a little fun," Dante says.

I bite down on my tongue. I don't want to talk about Serene. That conversation is off-limits. "No." I can't even imagine fucking Paige.

No, that's not true. It's easy to imagine hiking her skirt up and tearing her panties, fucking her in the hallway for the guards to watch as I make her scream my name.

But she's my employee and my daughter's nanny.

I have to keep it in my pants, if not for myself, then for Nova. She can't lose another nanny, not again.

Neither can I.

We have cameras throughout the house, especially in the playroom. I pull up the feed to watch Paige with my daughter.

The two of them are playing tea party, immersed in a world of make-believe. At least Nova has a new friend to play with during the day when Luca is at school.

I yank out my phone and shoot a quick text to Paige.

The job is yours. Don't screw this up. Nova is counting on you. We both are.

She glances down at her phone but doesn't answer my text.

There's a defiant streak in her. I can see it behind those glistening green eyes.

My cock twitches in my trousers.

Shit.

Hell no.

She's my daughter's nanny. Fucking her is not going to happen.

She runs a hand through her light brown hair, her long locks get slightly messy, and it makes her look that much more sexy and irresistible. She has natural streaks of blonde that frame her face, probably from being in the sun.

"Still watching the feed?" Dante chuckles as he glances over my shoulder.

I clear my throat.

Baseball. Soccer. Winter snowflakes.

I'm just throwing clean, non-sexual thoughts through my mind to shut down my desires. Does it work?

Hell, no.

Exhaling a loud sigh, I down that mug of coffee and grab a second cup. Why do I think caffeine will help me?

"What's her story?" Dante asks. He perches himself at the edge of the table and folds his arms across his chest.

Dante's a few years younger and gruffer. His eyes are always dark, even when he tries to soften his gaze at his son, Luca.

"I wouldn't know."

"Bullshit," Dante says. "I know you did a background check on the pretty brunette. I would expect nothing less since you brought her into my home."

"Never married. Her mother died of cancer recently. She sold the preschool she owned to take care of her mother. According to records, she's neck deep in medical bills, sold her house, her belongings, everything to pay off the debt."

Dante pushes himself from the table and nods for me to follow him out of the kitchen.

I take my cup of coffee and trail just a few steps behind him. He strolls into the study and slinks into the nearby armchair. There's a built-in wood bookcase lined with hundreds of books that Nikki insisted on filling the shelves on one wall. Everything from children's books to read to the kids to romance novels for her private escape.

"You've both lost someone close," Dante says as he crosses his legs.

Are her wounds as raw as mine? It's not a contest.

For once, he's trying not to rip off the bloody bandage on a scar that he caused.

Serene died because Vance DeLuca ordered a hit on our family.

6

PAIGE

Nova and I spend the afternoon having a tea party together before I lead her out of the playroom.

Dante and Moreno are having a heated conversation across the hallway in another room. I can't quite make out what is being said. Only, their tones make me want to run in the other direction.

I steer clear of bothering either of them. I'm sure they're busy.

"How about we go to the park?" I say to Nova.

The guard at the front entrance has disappeared.

Good.

It was warm when we arrived, so Nova won't need a coat. I lead her out the front door and toward my car.

"You're going to need a car seat," I mutter to myself.

The front door swings open from behind.

"What are you doing?" Moreno bellows.

"I was going to take Nova to the park, but I need to borrow a car seat from your truck." I assume he has one buckled into the backseat.

He huffs out a loud breath. "Absolutely not. You're not taking her off the premises."

"What? Why not? Do you not trust me?" I ask.

"I don't know you." He grabs my car keys from my hand and pockets them. "Nova, get inside!" Moreno points to the door, demanding she return to the house.

She sulks and kicks her feet against the ground as she walks, dirtying her pristine white shoes. Eventually, Nova scuttles inside the foyer.

Moreno steps toward the house and slams the door shut, leaving the two of us to speak alone.

My stomach is doing somersaults.

His eyes darken as he steps closer, invading my personal space. "You aren't to take her off the property."

"Ever? No field trips or afternoons at the playground?" I can't believe how unreasonable he's being. Is he angry with Nova or with me?

"That's right." He folds his arms across his chest. "If you want to take her to the park, there's a nice garden through the kitchen that you can take her to visit."

I open my mouth to object, but he yanks the front door open. "Inside, now!"

I shiver at his tone. Maybe I should reconsider this job, but Nova needs me. She needs a nanny who is warm, kind, patient, and loving. I'm not sure Moreno, her father, is any of those things.

"You don't have to be so gruff," I mutter as I enter back inside the foyer.

Moreno slams the door shut, and the house vibrates.

Nova's bright baby blues are wide. She takes a step back and then runs back to the playroom.

"Nova!" Moreno shouts for her to return.

"I'll get her," I say and head for the playroom, wanting to get away from Moreno.

He grabs my wrist. "Not so fast." He yanks me back to his side. "You and I, we're not finished."

Are we not? I'd like to be done. I'd prefer not to continue any further conversations with Moreno, but somehow I think the decision isn't the least bit mine to make.

Nova drags her feet and steps out from the playroom, hugging one of her stuffed animals tight to her chest.

"Upstairs, Nova." Moreno points to the staircase.

Wordlessly, she climbs the stairs, and Moreno gestures for me to follow.

He lets go of me, and I exhale a breath, relieved of the reprieve. Any chance he'll leave me alone?

Nope.

He follows me up the stairs.

"I'll show you to your room," Moreno says.

I glance behind me. He's one step below me. "My bags are in my car," I say.

He has my keys.

"I'll have Leone retrieve your things and bring your luggage to your room."

"That's not necessary. I can grab my suitcase. There isn't much."

I took minimalism to an entirely new level when my mother passed. Everything I own is in my car: one suitcase, a knapsack, and a bag of toiletries. I sold everything else that I owned to cover the expenses that insurance didn't pay for.

"Good, then Leone won't have any trouble bringing it up to your room," Moreno says. He gestures with two fingers for me to keep walking.

Nova is already at the top of the staircase, waiting for me. Does she plan on showing me her bedroom?

It's still early to be tucking her into bed. Neither of us has had dinner yet. Would all of us eat together as a family?

Once I reach the top step, Moreno leads me down the hallway toward a door on the right-hand side. He turns the handle and opens it to reveal a queen-sized mattress. The room is rather plain of decoration, with bare white walls, but a dresser is by the picturesque windows.

"You are welcome to hang pictures or decorate the room however you'd like."

"Thank you." I didn't plan on doing much with the place. It was a room to crash in. That's all I cared about.

"You have your own private bathroom suite," Moreno says as he steps farther into the bedroom and opens the bathroom door. He flips on the light and then steps out and around the room toward another door. "You have an adjoining room with Nova. Should she need anything during the night, you will look after her."

Moreno opens the adjoining door.

Nova hurries into her room and spins around to face me, her hands together in front of her.

"Yes, of course," I say.

I follow Nova into her bedroom. Lavender curtains with yellow trim are pulled back to let the sunlight into the room. The window shades are wide open, cascading the bright yellow painted walls in a sunny glow.

"I like your room," I say and smile at Nova.

She quirks a sideways grin. It's the biggest smile that I've seen from her today. Her eyes soften and turn a warmer shade of cerulean.

"I'll have Leone bring dinner up to your room for the two of you," Moreno says as he retreats for the door.

"What?" Is he punishing us for my attempt at taking Nova off the premises and to the park?

"I have work to finish, and I don't need to deal with the two of you." Moreno slams the door shut on his exit out of the bedroom.

Nova stands in the doorway between our bedrooms.

"Is your father always this grumpy?" I ask.

She smiles and nods.

It's the first form of communication other than the faint smile that I've witnessed from her today. She waited until her father had left the room.

Is she afraid of him? I wouldn't blame her.

He likes to boss us around. Well, things are going to have to change.

7

MORENO

I instruct Leone to bring dinner up to Paige and Nova while I bury myself with Dante in his office.

Leone is also under orders not to let either of them leave their suite under any circumstances.

"How's Nova doing?" Dante asks, sipping his glass of whiskey. His eyes are dark, and he stares down at the amber liquid before gulping it down and pouring a second glass.

"With the new nanny? It's too soon to tell," I say and sit back in the chair across from Dante, sinking into the leather.

To say I'm exhausted, is an understatement. I can't remember the last time I slept through the night. It had to be before *her* death.

He's quiet, pensive as he stares down at the drink in his hand.

"What is it, boss?"

"I've tried to give Luca and Nikki as much of a normal life as possible. Maybe that should extend to Nova. She's a little too young for elementary school, but we can certainly afford to send her to a private preschool where she can interact with other children."

My jaw tightens at his suggestion. "Do you think that's a good idea?"

I want what's best for my daughter. I don't need anyone, not even Don Ricci, telling me what I should be doing for Nova.

"Baby steps," Dante says. "I overheard the argument you had with the new nanny. Have her take Leone with them and let the kid get some fresh air. Maybe Nova will make a few friends her age at the park."

I can't believe his suggestion.

"Vance DeLuca is still out there!" I stand and pace the length of Dante's office. The room is hot, the air stuffy, and my stomach somersaults. I loosen my tie and wipe the sweat from my forehead.

Thankfully, I haven't eaten dinner, or I'd have brought it back up.

"We have no reason to believe that he's after Nova, and Leone will keep an eye on the nanny to ensure that she remains safe."

"Her name is Paige," I say. I'm not sure why, but I feel it necessary to correct him.

"You trust Paige with Nova, don't you?" Dante asks.

I wouldn't have hired her if I didn't trust that Nova would be in good hands. "Absolutely." That didn't mean I trusted anyone else around my kid.

"Then let them go to the park tomorrow. Nova could use the change of pace from this place."

A sharp, crisp knock against the frosted glass door interrupts us.

"Come in," Dante says.

Nikki pokes her head into the office. "Sorry to interrupt." Her eyes crinkle, and she offers a warm smile.

"Have a seat," Dante says to me and gestures to the chair that I had been in just a few minutes earlier.

I feel like they're about to tag team me. I'm just not sure why. I shut my mouth, jaw tight, and slump into the chair across from my boss. I clasp my hands together in my lap.

"Yes?" I'm waiting for whatever they are going to spring on me.

Do they not like the nanny I hired? Is she too hot?

Trust me, I noticed. That wasn't the reason I hired her, but it is certainly a perk.

"I'm worried about Nova," Nikki says. She folds her hands together in front of her and glances at Dante.

"I know. I think the new nanny, Paige, will be a good fit," I say. I'm still pissed about her trying to take Nova off the premises, but I don't believe her intentions were ill-willed.

"We are all worried about your daughter, and while I'm relieved you have hired a new nanny to entertain her, she needs a little more than what Paige can offer her. She needs to speak with a child psychologist," Dante says.

I laugh at his suggestion. "Nova doesn't speak." Did he hit his head?

Nikki steps closer and rests a hand on my arm. "Child psychologists are trained to work with young children, and there are other ways to get Nova to communicate, like with artwork."

"And you both think this is a good idea?" Our world is masked in secrets. What if Nova lets one of them escape?

Not to mention, I've seen her artwork. It's adorable and all, but she's four. It's not as though the therapist is going to gain much from a bunch of scribbles.

Dante clears his throat. "Yes, I believe this is best for Nova, and while I'm not thrilled to bring in an outsider, this woman comes highly recommended. We've done a thorough background check to ensure there is no connection to the DeLucas or anyone else of concern." He rests his hands on the desk. "What do you say?"

I don't think they'll let me say no. There isn't much of a choice, and I want what is best for my daughter.

"Yeah, sure."

"Good, because I've already made the appointment," Nikki says and digs into her pocket to hand me a business card.

I glance down at the card and the appointment scribbled on the back for this Friday afternoon.

"Looks like I'll be needing off for a few hours, boss." I offer a weak smile, trying to make light of the situation. It's all that I can do.

I want to pawn this task off on the new nanny. Let Paige run Nova around town so that I don't have to explain any part of the situation to the therapist.

But that's not how this works.

I'm not an idiot.

I keep my shit bottled up inside me.

Talking doesn't help, but I can't ignore the dark cloud looming over my little girl.

Something must be done before the trauma that she's suffered is irreversible.

I just hope it's not already too late.

8

PAIGE

I'm startled awake by the soft tapping of little Nova.

"Hey, good morning."

She stands beside my bed, her stuffed giraffe tight in one arm and her thumb tucked in her mouth.

"Do you want to keep me company?" I ask and pat the bed beside me.

I haven't glanced at the clock yet. The sun is just rising, and it's peeking through the curtains, which means it's too early for me to be awake.

Nova climbs atop my covers. She lies beside me for a split second before gathering onto her knees and tapping my shoulder again.

I roll onto my side.

She's not going to let me sleep. "Are you hungry for breakfast?"

Her eyes are wide, and she nods vigorously as if she's starving.

We had a feast for dinner. The guard brought our meal up to the bedroom, where the two of us opted for a picnic on the floor with her stuffed animals.

Hopefully, we can sneak down to the kitchen without bothering Moreno.

I want to check out the rest of the house, too.

"Let's get you dressed," I say and climb out from beneath the covers.

The pitter-patter of her feet hurries across the hardwood floor and to the open adjoining door. Nova heads inside, waiting for me to accompany her.

It takes a few seconds for me to fully wake. I rub the sleep from my eyes and catch sight of Nova poking her head around the corner of her door.

She's waiting for me, wondering if I'm coming. I head into her bedroom and grab a white dress with red poppies for her to wear. It's a summer dress, but it'll be perfect for today's weather.

"How about this?" I ask, showing her the outfit from her dresser.

She grins and snatches the fabric from my grip. "If you want to dress, I'll get ready too."

I don't sense any hesitation, so I head out through the adjoining door and close it most of the way.

My bag is situated on the floor by the dresser. I didn't bother to unpack my clothes or the few belongings that I own. I wasn't in the mood when Leone brought my things up to my room last night.

It's not like there's much to unpack, either.

Bending down, I unzip my duffel bag and grab a floral yellow and blue dress with cap sleeves and a keyhole in the front. It's knee-length and one of my favorite comfy dresses. I hold the accompanying undergarments and head to the bathroom, closing the door behind myself.

But there's no lock.

Great.

Hopefully, Nova won't burst through the door unannounced.

I doubt she'd knock, and she certainly isn't going to say a word to warn me she's coming into the room.

I hurry to undress from my pajamas and slip the dress over my head, tying the front to tighten the keyhole bodice. It's cute, light, and hugs my figure. Not that I should care. I'm not mixing business and pleasure.

I run my fingers through my hair before opening the bathroom door.

Nova is seated at the edge of my bed, her legs kicking wildly into the air. She's humming a lullaby and stops abruptly when she glances up at me.

Caught.

It's the first sound I've heard her make.

Was it a song her mother used to sing to her, or a previous nanny?

I doubt Moreno ever sang Nova any lullabies. He doesn't seem the type.

"Are you ready to go downstairs?" I ask.

She climbs down from the bed, the only indication of her answer. Nova doesn't smile. There's not even a slight nod of understanding. But I know she comprehends every word I say.

Maybe introducing her to sign language would be beneficial for her to communicate. Although I don't know very many words, we could learn together.

But the fact she was just humming a lullaby, I can't help the nagging feeling there's more than Moreno is telling me.

I turn the handle of the bedroom door, and it squeaks open. Leone is standing guard outside my room.

"Can I help you?" he asks.

"I'm taking Nova downstairs for breakfast," I say. I'm not asking his permission. This is her house, and she should be allowed to roam freely inside. Besides, her playroom is downstairs, and I can't imagine we'll be forced to have every meal upstairs in the bedroom.

I assume last night was a warning from Moreno for trying to take Nova off the property without permission.

He was right. As much as it kills me to admit it, I'd been with her only a few hours and shouldn't have planned to whisk her away to the park without speaking to her father.

"Very well, I'll show you to the kitchen," Leone says. He heads for the stairs.

Nova and I follow, a few steps back. She slips her hand into mine as we descend the stairs together.

I casually glance at her and catch a faint smile tugging at the corner of her lips. Good. At least we're getting along pretty well.

If only the same could be said about her father and me.

Leone leads me past the foyer and down to the kitchen on the opposite side of the house. The log cabin is vast.

"How long have you worked for Moreno?" I ask Leone, trying to make small talk.

He glances over his shoulder at me as he enters the kitchen and flips on the light. There's a high-top table in dark, rich wood with four chairs. The kitchen wasn't made for kids, but I'm confident Nova can sit there if I help her climb up on the chair.

"You mean Dante," Leone corrects me. "And it's been a minute."

Cryptic, as ever.

"Dante has a chef on staff. He'll be here in half an hour to prepare a lavish breakfast, but I'm guessing someone can't wait to eat?" Leone asks, glancing down at Nova.

She sneaks behind my legs.

"It's fine. I'm hungry too," I say. "I don't mind cooking for the two of us."

"Have at it, just don't make too big of a mess," Leone says as he heads out of the kitchen and guards the entrance of the kitchen beside the open entryway.

Is Moreno that concerned that I'm going to sneak off with his daughter that he's put a guard on me?

"Do you like pancakes?" I ask Nova and spin around to face the little girl.

She opens her mouth, eyes wide like she's about to speak, and then quickly shuts her lips. The pink lines of her lips are snapped closed and firm. Nova gives a slight glance toward the door and then a quick nod to respond.

I open the pantry and fiddle through, pleased to find pancake mix. At least I won't have to prepare it from scratch. I grab a bag of chocolate chips.

"What do you think, Nova? Do chocolate chips go in pancakes?" I show her the new bag, and she nods and jumps up and down excitedly.

"Inside," I gesture with my hand. "Or on top?"

"What are we making?" Moreno strolls into the kitchen and grabs the bag of chocolate chips from my hands.

"Breakfast," I say, stating the obvious.

He doesn't look the least bit amused. "With chocolate?"

"Ever heard of pancakes?" It's not like I'm giving her a chocolate bar for breakfast, though the look of disgust that crosses Moreno's face may as well suggest it.

He opens the pantry and puts the chocolate chips back inside.

"What are you doing?" I can't believe he thinks he can boss me around. Yes, he's her father and probably knows what's best for her, but it's one day with chocolate chip pancakes. It shouldn't be that big of a deal.

"Nova isn't eating chocolate for breakfast." He yanks open the refrigerator and pulls out a pint of blueberries. "Pop these in when you mix the batter."

I glance at Nova, pouty and wide-eyed, staring up at me, her head tilted to the side. I swear she's trying to convey to me to fight with her father for her to have chocolate, but I don't need to be in any more hot water.

"Great," I mutter under my breath with a fake smile. It's about all I can muster. "Where are the mixing bowls?" I don't know where anything is located in the massive kitchen, and while the pantry is obvious, there are dozens of cabinets. The bowls could be anywhere.

Moreno bends down and opens the cabinet beside the fridge, retrieving a metal bowl for me to mix the ingredients. "Silverware is in this drawer." He indicates to the drawer above the bowls. "And the spatula and whisk are over here."

"Thanks."

He opens the drawer and hands me a whisk before leaning back against the counter, folding his arms across his chest.

"Do you want me to make you a breakfast too?" I ask. I'm not sure why he's staring. It's nerve-wracking.

"That isn't necessary. Chef Savino will be in shortly. I did want to have a word with you alone," Moreno says.

Moreno opens the fridge, grabs a carafe of fresh orange juice and a plastic cup from the cabinet, bringing it to the table for Nova. He pours her a cup and pats the top of her head. "Did you sleep well?"

I mix the ingredients into the bowl, trying not to stare at the interaction between Moreno and his daughter. Her shoulders are tight, her body stiff.

Is she afraid of him?

He sighs and comes around the counter, perching himself at the edge. "I think you may be right, well, partially right." He is quick to clarify his position.

"About?"

Moreno glances over his shoulder at his daughter. "Nova could use a day at the park. Maybe interacting with other kids her age would be good for her. Luca is a sweet kid, but he's quite a bit older."

I can't help but grin. "That's good. She could use a few friends," I say. I get the feeling she doesn't play with anyone other than Luca, ordinarily.

"Maybe," Moreno says, "but you have to take Leone with you."

"What? Why?" Is he crazy? Leone will scare off everyone at the park, especially any friends Nova could potentially make.

"Being a businessman means that my family is easily a target. I can't take the chance that something will happen to Nova. You do understand, don't you?" Moreno asks.

I don't, but I smile and nod. "Yeah, sure." If he wants me to let some guard tag along, fine.

"Leone will drive you both to the park and anywhere else that you think is educational," Moreno says. "I want my daughter to have a well-rounded upbringing before her schooling begins."

I drop the spoon into the mixing bowl and step closer to Moreno. Something feels off. Like he's trying too hard.

"What's going on?" I stare into his darkened gaze, unwilling to glance away. If I'm looking after his daughter, he needs to tell me the truth. I can't go in blind and risk something happening to her.

Moreno clears his throat and skirts away from me. "Nothing that you need to concern yourself with, Nanny."

I scoff under my breath. "It's Paige," I correct him. "Unless you'd prefer me to call you Nova's father or Businessman?"

His jaw is tight, and he shoves his hands into his pants pockets. He's already dressed for the day, suit and tie. "Point taken."

When he doesn't divulge anything further, I back off and return to the mixing bowl. I drop in a handful of blueberries. "Are you going to tell me why the sudden change of heart?"

He stares at me blankly, like he has no idea what I'm talking about.

"Allowing me to take Nova to the park. Yesterday, you were one hundred percent against it. Today, you're letting us go, with a chaperone, pretty much wherever we'd like." It's hard not to find the sudden shift in his demeanor strange.

He clears his throat and averts his stare, his focus on the floor beside where I stand. "I made an appointment for Nova to see a doctor this Friday. I'm just trying to get ahead of things."

Doctor?

Moreno grabs a frying pan from another cabinet below and grabs the oil, giving me a hand.

Maybe he's just using it as a distraction, but I'm appreciative of the help.

"Is everything all right? If she has a health concern, Moreno, I need to be kept in the loop and made aware of any issues, allergies, anything that might affect her while we're together."

"It's not that kind of doctor," he says, keeping his voice low and just between the two of us.

I'm not sure I know where he's going with this conversation.

"A child psychologist was recommended to me, and I thought it would be good to have someone for her to talk to." Moreno winces at his choice of words.

"Oh. Okay. That's good," I say, trying to offer my support.

"Anyway, I'm sure she'll suggest that she try to make friends, engage with other kids her age, that sort of thing. I may as well let you take her to the park."

I breathe a sigh of relief. "Thank you."

Moreno pushes his heels forward and brushes past me, the conversation done for him. "Nova prefers her pancakes to be silver dollars."

"Thanks."

He heads out of the kitchen without another word.

I turn the stove down and bring the batter over. "Silver dollar," I hold up one finger, "or Mickey Mouse pancakes?" I ask Nova, holding up a second finger.

She holds up two fingers and then puts her hands to her head to make Mickey ears.

"Do you want chocolate chips on top?" I ask Nova, already knowing the answer.

Moreno isn't around. What he doesn't know won't hurt him.

Nova's eyes light up. With the widest grin, she points at the cabinet where her father put the chocolate chips.

Besides, it's not as though she's telling him anything.

9

PAIGE

After breakfast, Leone shuttles Nova and me to the park. It's quite a drive away from the picturesque cabin and gorgeous scenery.

Although we aren't anywhere near a big city, there is a park, playground, and a few shops across the street. We're as close to "downtown" as it comes in Breckenridge.

I grab a seat on the empty wooden bench and keep a close watch on Nova as she scuttles toward the sandbox.

"You don't have to shadow me," I say to Leone. He's towering behind me. I can feel his presence, and not only because he's blocking the sun.

I rather like the sunlight, the warm air, the fact it's summer. It won't last much longer, the nice weather.

Winter in Breckenridge is brutal. I'm not the least bit looking forward to it, although the thought of taking Nova sledding is slightly appealing.

"I'm supposed to make sure that Nova is safe."

I glance over my shoulder at the guard dressed in a sharp suit. "You stand out. Go over there." I gesture to the opposite side of the park.

"Why?" Leone asks. He pulls out a pair of sunglasses from his breast pocket. As if that will make him look calm and inconspicuous.

Now he just looks like a weirdo at the park.

"I'd like the opportunity to meet other nannies or mothers so that Nova can make some friends. With you hovering, no one is going to come over here."

He's probably hanging over my shoulder so mothers don't call the police reporting a pervert watching their kids.

I can't blame them. I'd be the first to call.

In fact, maybe if I can get him away from me, I can phone in an anonymous report.

It's cruel, but I'm already tired of a chaperone. And I'm not attracted to him, so any bodyguard fantasies are non-existent.

Moreno has more of a look of a bodyguard and protector than Leone.

Maybe it's the tattoos Moreno has that give him the bad boy vibe.

I shouldn't be attracted to him, but I am.

Leone struts around the bench and folds his arms across his chest as he goes to stand near the park entrance.

Good. At least I have a few minutes to myself.

Nova stands from the sandbox and hurries up the stairs to the slide. She doesn't look the least bit afraid. When she's playing, she appears without a care in the world.

That's how it should be.

Always.

"Is this seat taken?"

"Please," I say and gesture to the empty seat beside me on the bench.

Her two girls tear off for the swings. They're quite a bit older than Nova, but still in elementary school. At least they would be if it wasn't summer.

Luca is lucky enough to be involved in summer camp during the weekdays, which keeps him out of the house and busy with other kids his age.

"I'm Paige," I say, introducing myself to the brunette seated beside me.

"It's nice to meet you, Paige. I'm Ariella. And that is Olivia," she says, pointing toward the younger of her two daughters, "and Izzie. Let me guess. You're the new nanny for the Ricci family."

Was it that obvious that I was in over my head? "How did you know?"

"The bodyguard is kind of a dead giveaway," Ariella says with a laugh. "I mean, I get it. You should have someone shadowing you around, especially after what happened to her mother."

My mouth feels dry, and while I want to glance at Ariella, I can't take my eyes off Nova. The afternoon sun is sweltering, and sweat coats my brow. "What do you mean?" I choke out.

Moreno hadn't mentioned Nova's mother at all, and I didn't want to pry. It wasn't any of my business.

"Shit," Ariella mutters under her breath. "I don't mean to worry you. I'm sure you and Nova will be perfectly fine."

"You know Nova?" I catch a sideways glance at Ariella. She's biting on her bottom lip and doesn't look the least bit pleased that she opened her mouth.

Well, now she can't just shut it.

"What happened to her mother?" I ask. "Moreno hasn't so much as mentioned her."

Ariella glances at Leone and then back at the playground. "Can't say for certain. She went missing and turned up dead in the river. I wouldn't even say anything, but you should know what you're getting yourself involved with. Who the Ricci family is. Nova is a sweet girl, but I get the distinct feeling she needs someone to look after her."

Moreno was a businessman. Right? Tragically, his wife passed, but that didn't negate the fact he needed someone to care for his daughter. "That's why Moreno hired me."

"Of course," Ariella says.

Leone removes his sunglasses and strolls over toward us.

"Listen, I'll give you my number. If you need anything at all, call, text, it doesn't matter what time of day or night it is."

"That's very kind of you," I say.

She grabs a scrap of paper from her purse and scribbles down her digits before thrusting it into my hand. "Nova is a good kid. She deserves a lot better than the current hand she's been dealt. She used to yammer on about butterflies and fairies. Sweet as can be."

Nova didn't talk.

At least that's what her father had said.

Why was Moreno lying?

Ariella has no reason to lie to me and the fact she was humming a lullaby, something is amiss.

What had happened that made Nova refuse to speak?

10

MORENO

"Boss," Leone interrupts Dante and me as we're discussing our latest shipment of weapons.

The goods are late again, and I'm beginning to suspect the DeLucas are interfering, but I don't have proof of it yet.

"Come in." Dante gestures him into his office.

I'm situated across from Dante as he's seated behind his desk.

"What can we do for you?" Dante asks. "Did everything go smoothly today with the new nanny?"

"I wanted to speak with Moreno about what happened at the park." Leone comes farther into the

Chapter 10
73

office and shuts the door behind himself. The room is soundproof, offering absolute privacy.

I swallow the lump in my throat. "Did Nova have a problem with one of the other kids?" She hasn't been around too many children. If I don't count Luca, she hasn't been around anyone else's kids since the incident.

"It wasn't Nova," Leone says. "There was a woman with long dark hair. She was talking with the nanny for a few minutes. I didn't recognize her, but I have the distinct impression that she knew who we were."

"Good," I say and give a mere shrug.

We've worked hard to earn our reputation. As second to Dante, I'm proud of the Ricci Family and what we've managed to achieve over the last few years.

"Let's listen to him," Dante says, suggesting that I let the boss take the reins.

That's fine with me.

He's boss.

Leone shoves his hands into his pants pockets. "I don't have anything further to report. They spoke for a few minutes, exchanged numbers, it appears, and then I approached the two of them, which ended anything more than chitchat."

"I don't see the problem," I say and fold my hands behind my head.

Dante shoots me a glare. "The problem is that Serene used to take Nova to the park. The mothers are bound to gossip about why the chatty little tiger has suddenly lost her voice."

I'm not an idiot. I realize it's bound to come up with Paige, and I was just hoping it wouldn't be the first week of her employment.

I didn't even want to let her go to the park. Dante and Nikki had pushed the idea of Nova seeing a child psychologist, which encouraged me to give both girls more freedom.

That was a mistake.

I clear my throat and feel both of their harsh stares. "I'll deal with it."

"I'm sure you will," Dante says with bemusement. "Might I suggest you have a talk with her someplace with a lot of room and wide-open space?"

"Why?" I don't get where he's going with this line of thinking.

"She's going to feel trapped when she realizes the hit on our family. Take her someplace safe, remote, but romantic."

I snort under my breath. "Are you trying to hook me up with the nanny?"

Dante gestures for Leone to leave us alone.

I'd rather Leone didn't leave right now, but Dante is the boss. What he says goes.

Except I'm not going to fuck the nanny because Dante thinks I should.

"It's been nearly a year since your wife died. I think you deserve a little happiness, and if it involves letting her drop down to her knees to blow you, then I don't see the problem."

"Do you have to be so crass?" I run a hand through my hair, uncomfortable with the discussion. I'm not looking for sex or no strings attached. I've got a kid.

I need a mother more than I need a wife right now.

But I'm not marrying the nanny or fucking her. Though the thought has crossed my mind.

How could it not? She is perfect, every curve is well-pronounced, and she wears it with confidence, making her even sexier.

"I just think you'd be a lot happier if you were getting laid," Dante says as his lips curve into a grin.

He's not wrong, but I can't go down that path with Paige. It's dangerous for a variety of reasons.

"You wouldn't believe all the stuff Nikki and I have done. I always thought having a kid would slow down the libido but damn, it's like every week she wants to try something new."

"And you're complaining?" I don't believe him. He lights up whenever Nikki waltzes into the room.

"No," he says and laughs. "I'm just happy, and I want you to be happy, too. You don't have to lay the nanny. There are plenty of other hotties at the bar."

"I'm not going to a bar or club." I was too old to be chasing ass, even if Dante owned the place. It wasn't my style. I don't like to drink, and I feel out of place with everyone else getting trashed.

"Right. Strait-laced mafia, who'd have thought?" Dante teases.

I want to slug him, but it's only because we're family. I love the guy and hate him at the same time.

Family.

———

I loosen my tie and head up to my bedroom, but not before walking past Paige's bedroom. It's late. The door is shut, and Leone is standing guard.

"Don't you ever sleep?" I joke with him.

He looks like hell. I don't imagine she's making his life easy.

"Dante has me covering until Rhys gets back."

"Lucky you. Any problems?" I don't expect any, but Leone won't lie to me, whereas I'm not sure if Paige would tell me the truth about Nova's behavior.

Leone rolls his eyes. "Quiet as a mouse. Were you expecting something else, Moreno?"

I glance at my watch. It's well past when Nova should be in bed. I strut past Paige's bedroom and quietly turn the handle to Nova's room. The door opens without so much as a squeak.

There's a nightlight beside the bed that casts a warm glow across Nova's sleeping features. I tiptoe into her bedroom, fix the blanket that is half-strewn off the mattress, and bend down to kiss her cheek.

She doesn't stir. Nova is out cold.

The adjoining bedroom door is wide open, and I stalk across the bedroom toward the nanny's quarters. Her room is dark. I don't expect her to be awake. I really shouldn't be poking my head into her room, but I can't stop myself.

One glance, and she's staring back at me with those evergreen eyes.

Caught.

She's got an eBook reader in her hands, the soft glow lights up her features, and she places the tablet onto the bed.

"Sir?" Paige sits up straighter in bed, pulling the covers up around herself.

I clear my throat. I hadn't expected her to be awake. The bedroom lights were off, but that was probably to help Nova sleep and not disturb her.

I should retreat from the entrance to her bedroom, but my feet betray me. I gently close the adjoining door as I step closer to her bed, leaving the two of us completely alone.

"I wanted to ask how Nova has been doing. You both went to the park this afternoon." We should be having this conversation alone in the morning or while we're both dressed. Not when Paige is ready for bed.

She doesn't seem to mind. Or if she does, she's polite enough not to address the fact that I've come in unannounced. It's her only bit of free time and I'm the bastard stealing it from her.

Paige reaches for the bedside lamp and flips the switch. She squints for a moment at the bright light.

We both do.

I perch myself at the edge of the mattress. I don't ask her if I can sit.

She turned on the light to indicate that she's willing to talk with me. That's all the encouragement I need.

"Are you asking because you want to know how your daughter is doing, or is this about the girl I met at the park?"

11

PAIGE

I probably shouldn't have brought up meeting Ariella at the park, but I'm sure that Moreno already knows that we met. Isn't that why he has his men follow us around?

There's not a moment of privacy inside or beyond these four walls.

His eyes tighten, and I pull the covers tighter around myself. My nightgown is too thin for his heated stare. I should have worn sweats to bed, something less suggestive and revealing.

"Do you make it a habit of visiting all your nannies late at night by sneaking into their bedroom?"

A darkness looms over him at my words. Did I hit a nerve?

"I was always faithful to my wife," Moreno bellows. His words hit me like a slap to my face, and he stands.

I've insulted him.

Well, he probably shouldn't have come into my bedroom unannounced.

He needs to learn a little respect. Just because I work for him, doesn't mean he owns me. He can't just strut into my bedroom without permission.

"Sorry," I apologize. "But can't we have this conversation tomorrow?" I glance at the clock. It's just after nine o'clock. It's not really that late. I'm in bed early because entertaining Nova is exhausting.

Not that I want to admit that to Moreno.

"No." His tone is clipped. "Get dressed and meet me downstairs."

Moreno wordlessly stands and exits out of my bedroom through the main door.

What the hell just happened?

I sit and stare at the door for a few seconds before pushing myself out of bed and obliging his request. Why do I need to get dressed?

I grumble under my breath and grab a pair of sweats and a t-shirt.

We're not going anywhere, right?

I hurry into the bathroom, dress, and then quietly head out of the bedroom.

I'm surprised—and relieved—there isn't a guard standing outside the door. Maybe Moreno is beginning to trust me. I *am* watching his daughter.

I head down the hallway, and he's waiting for me at the bottom of the stairwell.

"Took you long enough." Moreno's brow furrows. "That outfit won't do. Go back and change into something that you'd wear out of the house."

I glance down at my comfortable clothes. "I would wear this out," I mutter under my breath. It's not exactly fashionable or cute, but does it need to be?

He's still in his midnight black suit that he wore today, suit, tie and all.

I'm about ready to act like his daughter and throw a temper tantrum, but exhale a heavy breath instead.

"Fine." I head back to the bedroom and shut the door.

I don't have anything super fancy other than my interview suit, and I'm not wearing that for whatever he has planned.

Footsteps are heading up the stairwell. Moreno must be coming upstairs.

Does he intend on helping me pick something out?

Why?

I grab a black knee-length skirt and dark red blouse. I don't know what all the fuss is about. Moreno has a stick shoved up his butt.

I snicker and, with a sly smile, quickly change clothes in the bathroom. When I open the bedroom door, Moreno stands on the opposite side and glances me up and down.

It's quite apparent that he approves.

His gaze on my body brings a forbidden heat to my cheeks.

"Where are we going?" I ask, closing the door behind myself.

He leads me down the stairs to the foyer, where I put on my shoes. He grabs the keys to his vehicle.

"I thought you could use a night out, and it's an opportunity for us to get to know one another. Unless you have other plans?"

I laugh under my breath as I slip into my black heels. "You mean other than reading before bed?" I like my nightly routine, but going out isn't a bad decision, either. I want to know more about Nova's mother, and what better person to tell me than Moreno?

He opens the front door and leads me outside to his fancy sports car.

"Nice ride," I say. I followed his SUV the other day up to the cabin. "You have more than one car?"

Moreno hits the buttons to unlock the passenger door and opens it for me. "This is the boss's car, but I like borrowing it any chance I get."

Well, at least he's honest.

Moreno waits for me to climb in before closing the door behind me.

"Thank you," I say and buckle up while he hurries around to the driver's side.

I feel awkward, like this is a date. Except, it isn't supposed to be anything more than a boss and his employee going out.

I shouldn't be doing this, mixing business with pleasure, but maybe I'm reading into the offer to take me out?

He isn't interested in me.

Moreno has given no indication that he likes me.

He tolerates me, but that's the extent of his desire toward me.

I care for his daughter, and any kindness he's showing is because of Nova.

"Where are we going?" I ask again, relaxing as the engine purrs and we whip onto the road, and the gates are opened before we even approach.

"Out for drinks. You do drink?"

"Yes," I say.

The car is a manual, and Moreno rolls out the gears as we tear down the road. My stomach is a tangle of knots.

He downshifts as we ease down the road. The sunset is late in summer, and the sky is still lit up, and it's well after nine at night. "I forgot how long it stays light up here," I say.

"Yeah, I guess it does. I hate to admit I haven't noticed. I'm usually cooped up at the house most nights." Moreno glances at me briefly before returning his attention on the road.

"Dante keeps you busy?"

His grip tightens on the steering wheel.

"Work keeps me busy," Moreno says.

"You never told me what you do for a living." I doubt he'll open up to me, but it's worth a shot.

Moreno shifts in his seat. He reaches for his tie and tugs on it to loosen the fabric. "Are you hot?" he asks and turns up the air conditioning.

It's a little warm, but it doesn't bother me.

Sweat is sticking to his brow, and I'm not sure if it's my question or the warm August air baking the car.

"Make yourself comfortable. It's your car," I say.

"Yeah," he says and adjusts the thermostat on the vehicle.

He still hasn't answered my question. I'm not letting it go. Not yet. "You were saying about what you do for a living."

"I'm a businessman."

Cryptic. I could have guessed that answer based on his suit. He's dressed nice and sharp. It's obvious he's not a realtor, and I haven't seen him out of the house long enough to be a lawyer.

"That's like code for a hitman," I joke.

Moreno gives me a long side glare.

Shit.

He doesn't look the least bit amused by my remark.

"Wait. You don't really kill people for a living?" My stomach sinks, like it's about to hit the floor.

"I'm not a hired assassin," Moreno says.

I breathe a sigh of relief. "Oh, good. I'd hate to have to explain to Nova what her father does for a living."

He rolls the gears back up as we breeze out of town.

"I thought we were going for drinks," I say.

"You ask too many questions."

Cryptic as ever.

Where the hell is he taking me?

12

MORENO

Hitman? Did she say she thinks I kill people for a living? I'm tired, but I didn't imagine her question.

The girl wreaks of trouble.

Fuck.

Yes, I've killed men, but it's not like I signed up to murder a snitch. It's part of the responsibility of being a second to Dante.

Not that the pretty little nanny needs to know any of that. It's better if she's kept in the dark. It's safer for her and my family.

"Where are we going?" Paige asks again, and this time there's a quiver in her voice.

"I told you, drinks." It's not like I drink. I stay away from liquor, but I'm used to being Dante's chaperone. At least when he used to go out and pick up pretty girls. That was before he met Nikki and knocked her up.

I won't make that same mistake.

Not that Dante isn't happy, he's madly in love with the girl he slept with, but it was against his better judgment to sleep with the daughter of his enemy.

I've at least got a little class.

I don't plan on bedding the nanny.

I glance at her out of the corner of my eye and then return my attention to the road. The car feels stuffy, and although I've already loosened my tie, it doesn't do enough to chill the vehicle down.

"Are you always this cryptic?" Paige asks.

The quiver is gone from her voice. Her hands are positioned in her lap. She looks calm and collected.

Is it an act?

Can she see right through me and the kind of man that I am?

"Comes with the job of working for Dante," I say and laugh under my breath. She has no idea of the secrets I'm forced to keep.

"Like I said, cryptic." She stares at me, and I feel even warmer under her scrutiny.

Tonight, is about putting her on the hot seat, not the other way around. How the hell does she manage to tangle my insides into a knot?

It had to be the simple fact that she looks hot in that outfit.

Maybe I should have let her wear sweatpants and a t-shirt out tonight so I wouldn't be undressing her in my mind.

I haven't been laid since Serene's passing. Sleeping with any other woman felt wrong, like betraying my wife.

But she's dead, and I've been a miserable bastard for far too long.

I want just one taste of the sweet, forbidden fruit.

Paige is off-limits. She's my daughter's nanny, but that doesn't stop me from enjoying being around her. And imagining what it would be like to kiss her, touch her, and drive my cock inside her.

"We're almost at the place," I say and pull off the main road to a nightclub. It's low-key for the middle of the week, without too many patrons.

Perfect.

Dante owns quite a few clubs and bars in Breckenridge and outside of town. I opted for the more elusive and classier location, Spring Valley. Paige strikes me as the kind of girl who likes to be wined and dined.

I pull up out front and valet the vehicle, handing the keys over to the attendant on duty. "Sir, it's good to see you again."

I offer him the keys and a twenty, and the young man hands me a ticket for the valet. Not that I need it. Everyone who works here knows who I am. While Dante owns the club, I've helped manage it, handle the hires, and deal with the problems that arise from time to time.

Paige raises an inquisitive eyebrow and leans into me. Her body grazes against mine as she leans in to whisper into my ear, "I can't believe you let them valet your car."

"Dante's car," I correct her with a sly grin.

"Sir," the bouncer gives the nod and opens the door of us.

I wrap my arm around Paige's waist as I lead her inside, past the bouncer, claiming her as my own. If he so much as looks at her the wrong way, he's dead.

The bouncer doesn't ask for either of our identifications. We look well past twenty-one, and he's also not going to bother me if he wants to keep his precious job.

Her eyes rake over the inside of the club. Pulse-pounding music reverberates against the walls as I lead her back toward the VIP lounge.

"Fancy," she says as I push back the plush cranberry velvet curtain.

I secure the curtain back so that we aren't hidden away. There aren't too many guests tonight, and I didn't bring her here to fuck her. If I'd have wanted to do that, we could have done so in her bedroom.

There's a long sofa and a glass table situated low on the ground. I sit down and Paige sits beside me but leaves ample space between us.

I should have let her sit down first so I could scoot closer. I'll rectify that mistake before the night is over.

Hell, before she's finished her first drink for the night.

The newest hire, Ashlee, who barely looks twenty-one, saunters over toward us. "Can I get you both drinks?"

"Long Island Iced Tea," Paige says.

"I'll have my usual," I say.

Ashlee gives a brief nod and a smile and hurries out of the VIP lounge. She's short and blonde, cute, but not my type. Ashlee is too young. I prefer a woman with more life experience than straight out of high school and eager to please any man she can get her claws into.

I shift on the sofa, turning to face Paige, and rest my arm on the back of the chair. I can easily caress her neck if I let my fingers wander, but I don't.

Not yet.

It's tempting, but she's not mine.

At least not yet.

I want to make her mine and hear her beg for me to bring her pleasure.

"Let's talk," I say as I stare into Paige's mesmerizing gaze. "You met a mother at the park."

Let her think I'm trying to make small talk.

Ashlee is quick to return with our drinks and places them on the glass table. I lean forward to grab my Coke and, in the process, scoot closer toward Paige.

"Is this why you brought me out? To liquor me up so I'd talk to you about Ariella?" She reaches for her drink and brings the glass to her lips.

I quirk a sideways grin. "You've figured me out."

What I want to know is what that brat Ariella told Paige about my family.

I don't let on that I intend on staying completely sober, and while I have no intention of physically taking advantage of her, I will get her to tell me everything.

"Yeah, well, it wasn't that hard," Paige says. She sips her drink before placing the glass back on the table. "And yes, I met a mom at the playground. Not a surprise. Although I do have a few questions for you."

"I would expect nothing less," I say. How much did she tell Paige about the Ricci family?

I don't know much about Ariella, but I am blatantly aware that she's married to one of those Eagle Tactical fellows, a real pain in my ass.

This means Paige's new friend needs to be kept away from the compound for her own good. I'd hate to have to ruin an innocent friendship with a bullet.

13

PAIGE

My Long Island Iced Tea is sweet and sharp at the same time. The place doesn't water down their liquor.

I let my heels slide off my feet and tuck my legs up beneath me on the plush sofa, shifting to face Moreno.

He isn't going to let the meeting between Ariella and me slide. His stupid bodyguard is a rat, as far as I'm concerned.

"No one's said anything about Nova's mother." I'm trying to tread carefully over a delicate topic. I don't want Moreno to know that I learned anything specific from my little chat with Ariella. "Where is she?" I ask. My voice is soft.

"I don't see how that's any of your concern."

I reach for my drink, wanting to feel a slight buzz to help me unwind. Moreno is domineering, and I imagine he's not just a grumpy boss to me.

Is he grumpy in bed too?

"I'm caring for Nova. It would help me relate to her and understand her situation better if I knew the whole story."

He must admit that I'm not wrong. If his daughter used to talk, then wouldn't he want her to speak again? What kind of parent wouldn't want what's best for their child?

If I push too hard, he's bound to recoil, or worse, fire my ass.

"Her mother isn't in the picture."

"No shit," I mutter under my breath.

Moreno's stare is dark and sends a chill down my spine.

"Excuse me?" he bellows.

My mouth feels like sandpaper, and I reach for my glass, desperate for another sip—something to quench my parched throat.

"My wife, Serene, was murdered, but I'm guessing you already knew that from your little friend."

I down the rest of my drink and place the empty glass on the table. "I'm sorry."

"Are you, because I have the feeling you have twenty more questions to go along with that one?"

He isn't wrong, but now I feel like a piece of shit asking him about his dead wife, what happened, and pretending that I wasn't aware the entire time. "I really am sorry. I didn't mean to upset you."

I reach for his arm and rest my hand atop his suit coat. I feel naked in my blouse and skirt compared to all the layers Moreno wears.

His brow is knitted tight, and his lips are pinched together. "I loved Serene. I still love her, but she's not here anymore, and we make do with the hand we're dealt."

Moreno reaches for his drink and stands, taking it with him, leaving me in the dust as he stalks off toward the bar.

Shit.

I didn't mean to offend him. I slip back on my heels and grab my glass. I step out of the VIP booth and down toward the main floor where the bar is situated.

Moreno leans forward, his hands clasped together on the bar as he speaks with Ashlee. I can only imagine what they're talking about. I want to run in the opposite direction.

Should I give him space?

Everything within me is screaming to go sit back down.

But my legs betray me as I step forward, one foot in front of the other.

I have to do something. I'm just not sure what.

Moreno is my boss. If I can't fix this, I'm royally screwed. It's not like after my work shift I can go home, unwind, and escape work.

I live with the man. And while we don't share a bedroom, we live under the same roof.

Talk about complicated.

I intentionally step a little louder as I approach, my heels clanking over the wooden floorboards, but the music is too loud for him to notice.

"I've never seen you order whiskey," Ashlee says as she pours him a fresh glass. "Hell, I've never seen you order alcohol."

Ashlee's eyes widen, and then she steps away to give us privacy.

I'm not sure whether to thank her or wrestle her back over to keep things civil between us.

"Can we talk about Nova?" My voice is soft, gentle, and non-threatening. I don't want to fight with him. I feel like he's a ticking time bomb and will explode at any second.

His silence scares me more than anything.

He downs his drink and gestures the bartender back over. "Just leave the bottle."

Ashlee grabs the top-shelf whiskey and leaves it on the counter before she's out of sight and earshot.

"What do you want to know?" Moreno asks, but his question comes out more like an accusation, and I have the sneaking suspicion if I ask what I'm desperate to find out, it's not going to end well.

"I noticed she doesn't have any friends."

He foregoes the glass for the second drink of whiskey and brings the bottle to his lips instead. "She has Luca."

"He's almost six," I remind him. "She needs friends her age."

He turns quickly to face me, and I can feel a warmth flood through me at his proximity. It doesn't stop there.

No, he steps closer, forcing me to take a small step back, except he grabs my hip and traps me between him and the bar.

I inhale a sharp breath.

"I let you take her to the park." There's no kindness in his words and no amount of warmth in his dark, stern gaze that towers down at me.

I don't push him away.

Maybe I should and head outside for some fresh air. The thought rattles through my brain, but it's gone when he lands his lips down on mine.

His breath is hot, fiery. His hands pull at my hips, clutching me against him. He's rough and demanding, but his forcefulness is met only with my eagerness.

"Moreno," I whisper, surprised by the single word that spills past my lips.

What are we doing?

Why is he kissing me?

His hand is positioned at my lower back. He pulls me tighter, letting me feel his desire as his other hand snakes down my thighs and up my skirt.

No. No. No.

He's my boss.

I shouldn't be doing this with him.

We shouldn't be doing this.

I'm lost in a sea of warmth and desire as his fingers tease me through my panties. "Someone could see us," I rasp against his lips.

Already, he's made me breathless.

"Do you want me to stop?" he whispers into my ear and begins to suck and tug on the bottom of my earlobe.

Fuck.

He knows exactly what to do to make me fall to pieces.

I'm weak at the knees, literally, and I'm not sure how much longer I can stand. Part of me considers hopping up on the bar to let him fuck me, but I know we're not alone.

It's just a fleeting fantasy. That can't happen.

Hell, this shouldn't be happening, but it is, and I don't stop him.

Moreno pulls back and glances down at my lips.

"Why'd you stop?" Already, I'm out of breath, panting and gasping for air as he withdraws his digits from beneath my skirt.

"You didn't beg me to let you come," Moreno says with a sly grin.

I want to wipe that smug smile off his face. Is this all a game to him?

I lean forward to kiss him, proving that I want him and I want this to happen between us.

"Moreno!" a booming voice carries through the bar. "Looks like you've found quite a charming replacement."

Embarrassment burns my cheeks. Did Vance see what we were doing?

The contract I signed with Nanny Agency, Inc. promised that I would be professional at all times.

Well, fuck.

"Vance DeLuca," Moreno's tone sends a shudder down my spine.

"Say hi to Nicole for me," Vance says with a wicked grin.

There's something dark and sinister about the way Vance moves toward Moreno.

"Don't move," Moreno warns me.

What? Why?

Where would I go?

I don't have the slightest clue what the hell is going on, but I can already sense trouble. These two men have a history together.

If they hate each other, then why did Moreno use Nanny Agency, Inc. to hire me?

I reach into my clutch and pull out my cell phone. My hands are shaking. I'm honestly not even sure who I would call. I don't have Dante's number, and the police can't help. I suspect by the time they'd show up, the bar will be in shambles, and Moreno will end up arrested along with the man who arranged for me to be hired as a nanny for the Riccis.

Moreno pulls back his arm and lands a forceful uppercut on Vance.

Then he grabs my arm and drags me hastily out of the bar and past the bouncer standing guard while we hurry to the car.

Valet already pulled the vehicle around. There's no waiting for his car, almost like they knew he'd be jetting out of here.

But how would they know that?

"What's going on?" I ask. I hurry into the car, and Moreno is already in the driver's seat by the time I'm buckling into my seat.

He hits the gas, and we fly out of the parking lot at record speed.

Moreno's jaw is tight, his hands white-knuckling the steering wheel. He keeps glancing in the rearview mirror, and we are whizzing by at record speed.

If we pass by a cop, Moreno is getting a ticket for reckless driving. His foot hasn't let up from the gas pedal as we whip around the curves of the road and head back toward town.

"Talk to me!"

I can't stand the silence.

Whatever he thinks I can't handle, he hasn't even tried to explain himself.

14

MORENO

I shouldn't have tried to kiss Paige.

Not that I regret thrusting my tongue into her mouth or my hand up her skirt. I could feel her tremble in my arms.

Paige's voice is filled with fear even now, as we rush back toward the complex. It's the only safe place for her, with dozens of men standing guard to protect our family.

That had been the mistake made the day that Serene died. She wasn't at home, safe.

And it had gotten her killed.

She wasn't the only one who died that day, murdered by Vance and his men.

"Talk to me!"

I want to tell her everything, but I doubt she can handle it, and letting her leave is no longer an option.

"Vance DeLuca is the head of the DeLuca family."

She's silent.

A little too silent. "They're mafia," I reiterate, having the suspicion that she doesn't know what I'm talking about. Why would she?

"And what does that have to do with Nikki? He mentioned Nicole too."

I exhale a heavy breath. It isn't my place to share Nikki's past with Paige. That's her story to tell. "They're old family," I say.

"Nikki is part of the mafia? I can't believe that," Paige says. Her hands are in her lap, and she's fiddling with her fingers, picking at her perfectly polished nails.

"Born into is more like it. A mafia princess."

"No way." Paige shakes her head in denial. "And you're okay living with them? With your daughter under their roof?"

Does she not realize I'm one of them?

I'm not a DeLuca. I'm a Ricci.

"Nikki isn't part of the DeLuca family anymore. She hasn't been since before Luca was born. Her father is dead, and Vance took over the business when she came to stay with us indefinitely."

It's more than I should confide in her.

"None of this is to be shared with anyone. Do you understand?" I shoot her a hard stare before returning my gaze to the road.

It's dark outside, the night air has finally cooled off, and the car is comfortable except for the thick tension between us.

"I won't say anything. Who would I tell?" Paige says. "Besides, who would even believe me?"

"I need to call Dante. Not a word. Okay?" I warn her before calling him through the car's Bluetooth system.

"What's up?" Dante answers on the first ring.

"We've got company," I say.

He's quick to respond. "Invited or uninvited?" He's silently asking whether we need reinforcements or I'm bringing home a date.

"Uninvited." I have Paige in the car with me. Who the hell else would I bring home or invite back with us? He should know me better than that.

"Figured as much. We'll be ready when you get here," Dante says.

I hang up the call and exhale a heavy breath.

Nova will be safe. She, Luca, and Nikki will be locked away in the panic room the minute Dante hangs up the phone.

There are protocols to follow. It doesn't matter that it's the middle of the night for Nova and Luca. They'll be pulled out of their beds and taken into the panic room to sleep.

"Now what?" Paige asks. She glances in the side mirror as a set of headlights are creeping up on us from behind.

It's not uncommon for others to be out on the road at this hour.

It's summer.

There are plenty of tourists traveling up to Glacier. The national park isn't that far from Breckenridge, and we get quite a few RVs driving through town.

But another glance in the rearview mirror, and it's not an RV.

The headlights are lower and closer together.

It's a car, but it's too dark and far away to ascertain any more information.

I hit the gas harder, revving the engine and rolling out the gears as we hurry back toward the compound.

If it is Vance, he's not coming without an entourage.

————

We hurry back through the main gate, and I usher Paige inside the house and up to the panic room. The entrance is hidden away in Dante and Nikki's master bedroom, inside the closet.

I punch in the code, and the door slowly swings open. "Get inside."

"Where's Nova?" Paige asks. She spins around on her heel, staring up at me.

"She's asleep in here," Nikki's soft voice answers from inside the panic room.

Does she honestly think I'd usher her inside and forget my daughter?

"What about you?" Paige hesitates. Her hand grips my arm, and I feel the slight tremble in her touch.

"I'll be fine. Someone has to protect you girls and the kids."

I lean down, stealing one more kiss in case the opportunity never comes again. I'm not sure whether Vance is on the way or not, but he didn't show up in Spring Valley at a club Dante owns by accident.

15

PAIGE

I still feel his breath against my lips, my heart hammering against my ribcage, as he pushes me inside the panic room and shuts the door.

We're locked inside.

Nikki sits on a futon sofa and shifts her legs to make room for me to join her. The room is small but furnished. There's a set of bunk beds against the wall. Luca is sleeping on the top bunk, and Nova is curled up beside Nikki on the sofa.

The moment I step into the room and head for the sofa, Nova's arms are outstretched for me.

"You're supposed to be asleep," I say and pull Nova into my arms for a hug as I sit down on the couch.

The little one climbs into my lap for cuddles, and Nikki hands me a throw blanket from the back of the futon that I can use to help make Nova a little more comfortable.

"Good luck getting her to sleep," Nikki says with a wayward grin. "First time in lockdown. I'm betting this isn't what you thought being a nanny was all about."

I chuckle under my breath. "Moreno certainly didn't mention a panic room."

"I'll bet he didn't." She laughs and shakes her head.

The room smells of fresh paint, new wood, and recent construction, unlike the remainder of the cabin, which seems to be kept up but is not new.

"I heard you had a hot date with the boss," Nikki says.

She has me rattled speechless, and Nova glances up at me, curious as to our conversation. Nova looks about as stressed as I feel.

"Relax, I'm just kidding. I'm sure you two just went out as friends to get to know one another."

I gently rub Nova's back to get her to settle in. She seems to take comfort in it and rests her head on my chest as she buries against me for cuddles.

"That was one hell of a kiss, though," Nikki says.

Did it get several degrees warmer in here?

Nova pokes her head up, staring at me.

For once, I'm grateful she doesn't speak. I'm not sure what she'd say about her father and me sharing a kiss.

She's four, though. It's not like she has any say in who her father dates.

Not that we're dating.

"Anyway," I say with an overly zealous grin, trying to change the subject. "Is this a regular occurrence?" I gesture at the panic room. How often should I get used to coming in here?

"Playing hide and please don't seek?" Nikki quips. "More often than I'd like, but it's honestly not that often. I think in the past year, since Dante had the room built, we've been in here twice."

That wasn't too bad.

"How much did Moreno tell you about why we're holed up in here?" Nikki asks.

She seems cautious, like she doesn't want to give more away than she's supposed to, but I get the distinct impression that if I can get the girl to talk, she'll talk up a storm. Already, she's said far more than I have since being cooped up together.

Maybe she'll spill all of Moreno's secrets.

"I met Vance at the club," I say, studying her expression. Maybe I shouldn't mention that he runs Nanny Agency, Inc..

The color drains out of her face. "He's back?" Nikki's tongue darts out as she licks her lips and stands.

She begins pacing the length of the room. It's not overly big, but we're also not in a closet.

Back?

When did he leave?

Nova's grip on me tightens.

I had hoped that she'd fallen to sleep or at least been growing close, but at the sound of Vance's name, she reacted just as Nikki had.

What was going on?

"He mentioned you," I say, staring up at Nikki. I probably should watch what I say around Nova, but it's not like I can put her in another room and have this conversation between just the adults. We're all locked in here together.

"Not a surprise. He's been trying to get to me since I ran away. Bastard thinks he can run my life even with my father dead and out of the picture." She folds her arms across her chest and slumps down onto the couch.

"No one is going to let anything happen to you or anyone here," I say.

"I know." Nikki's lips roll together tight as she shuts her mouth.

There's something she isn't saying.

She's not the only one keeping secrets.

———

"False alarm," Dante says as he unlocks the door to the panic room.

Moreno follows behind him, looking at the empty bottom bunk for Nova before realizing that she's in my arms, fast asleep.

I'd dozed off for a few minutes, or was it hours that had passed?

"It's late. We should get her to bed," Moreno says. He leans forward, scooping the sleeping child from my arms.

I silently stand and follow him out of the panic room.

I have more questions dancing through my head. The sun is already coming up, peeking through the curtains.

"Are you sure it's safe?" My eyes burn, and I rub at them while following behind Moreno as he tucks Nova into bed, pulling the covers tight around her small frame.

He bends down, pressing a kiss to her forehead before glancing over his shoulder at me.

"You should get some sleep. Nova will be up early."

I exhale a heavy breath. "That's not likely to happen. I'm surprised I fell asleep at all in there," I admit.

"I'm going to put on a pot of coffee. Do you want some?"

I follow him downstairs. He's already changed out of his suit. I'm not sure when he undressed, but I can't help but smile at the tight dark shirt and sweatpants that he has on.

I've never seen him looking the least bit casual, and it's just as sexy as when he's in his overpriced suit.

"Yeah, that sounds good." I'm on his heels, down that stairs, and take a seat at the high-top table in the kitchen.

Moreno grabs me a cup of coffee along with one for himself and comes to sit across from me.

He looks about as tired as I feel. "You don't have to stay up with me," I say.

I doubt that's the reason that he's still awake, but I don't want him to feel like he must keep an eye on me.

"The adrenaline is about as strong as four cups of coffee," Moreno says and smiles down at his mug.

"If that's the case, then I'll take this off your hands." I reach for his cup of coffee, but he snatches it away first.

Moreno offers a wry grin. "Nice try." His gaze falls back to his steaming hot drink. "Listen, I know you want to take Nova to the park and go out for adventures, but I can't let that continue anymore."

It was one outing.

I sip my drink. The liquid burns the roof of my mouth, and I wince.

"Is this because of Ariella or the guy at the club?" I'm not sure whether he's overprotective or controlling. I haven't gotten to know Moreno long enough to decipher between the two options yet.

Vance rates high on the creepy factor. I felt that way when I first met him, but I don't know if Moreno is overreacting or he's right.

Moreno places his mug down forcefully on the table.

It clanks, and I shiver involuntarily.

"Does it matter?" he asks.

It matters to me, but I don't think he'll give an honest answer.

"You can't keep Nova locked up inside this place."

His eyes tighten, and there's a darkness that settles over him as he speaks. "It's her home."

"She's not a prisoner. She's a child."

Moreno huffs loudly under his breath. "You can't leave, either."

"What?"

He can't be serious.

"Do you think it's safe for you out there? Vance knows you work for me. You're a target."

I open my mouth to tell him that Vance is the one running the nanny agency, but think better of it. Next, he'll no longer trust me and think that I work for Vance.

"We'll be fine. I'll bring Leone with me."

"You're not taking it seriously enough," Moreno says. His jaw is tight, and he steps away from the kitchen table and pours a second cup of coffee. "Exactly why you can't leave and certainly not with my daughter."

Another cup of coffee.

Yeah, that's exactly what he needs.

He's already wired.

"Fuck."

"What's wrong?" I glance back at him over my shoulder. He's studying his phone. Something pissed him off, and this time, it wasn't me.

16

MORENO

The fucking therapist appointment.

I almost forgot about it. Well, I wanted to forget about it because taking Nova to a shrink wasn't my idea.

I have Dante and Nikki to thank for interfering in my business.

They're trying to be helpful, looking out for the family, but that doesn't make it easier. I don't want to talk about Serene's death, but it's bound to come up.

There's an email from the therapist asking me to fill out this stupid form before the session. I thought it was insurance shit, wanting information for payment, and I have enough cash just to hand her hundreds to not deal with it, but one glance and I'm dead wrong.

She wants a detailed report on our family.

The therapist is requesting that both parents be at the appointment.

Fuck.

I thought Nikki handled that bit of information?

Apparently not.

"You want to get out of here with Nova?" I shoot Paige a look.

A terrible idea is floating through my mind. I shouldn't even suggest it.

She's hesitant to answer. It's no wonder. I've already demanded that she can't leave the premises with my daughter. "I thought the park was off-limits?"

I pour that second cup of coffee and let the hot, bitter liquid slide down my throat as I take a big gulp.

It is off-limits. I need her to accompany me to the therapist's office and not as the nanny. Nova isn't going to say a word, and Nikki would never go through with it.

Besides, it'll keep the questions to a minimum, and we won't have to talk about Serene's murder.

I'm sure as shit not ready to talk about it, and Nova doesn't speak.

Problem solved.

"I need you to come with me on Friday to an appointment for Nova."

Her brow furrows. "I don't understand."

How could she? I exhale a heavy sigh. How do I explain this without sounding like a complete asshole?

Who the fuck cares? I'm grieving, and she's my employee. She'll obey me.

"You'll be on the clock," I say. "I'll pay you overtime for accompanying me to Nova's therapy appointment, as her mother."

She laughs.

The audacity she has, to laugh at my pain. "You find this funny?"

The smile vanishes from her face and her complexion grows pale. "You're serious?"

Paige thought I was joking with her. I don't use humor as a crutch. "There are some things that I prefer to keep private. I require your services for Friday outside of the home with Nova. Is that a problem?"

Wordlessly, she shakes her head.

"What's that?"

"It's no problem," Paige says.

"Good." I finish the rest of my coffee and then dispose of the mug into the sink.

I hate the look that she's giving me. Does she feel sorry for me? I'm tired of the pity looks and constant regards from fellow family members after Serene's passing.

I still mourn the loss of my wife every single day.

I never thought I'd even consider moving on or thinking about a woman in any way other than platonically, but one glance at Paige, and I'm guilty.

I want her. My body wants her. And my heart is finally beating like I'm alive again.

But I can't have her. She's not mine.

Paige's gaze is on me, and I swear it's fueled with sadness and despair. She feels sorry for me. I can't take it. I hate those looks of pity.

I don't want a pity fuck.

I storm out of the kitchen, leaving her alone to finish her cup of coffee.

————

I've avoided Paige as best as I can. Mostly, I've avoided any conversation with her.

We have extra guards at the house and on the property to ensure the family is safe.

Paige hasn't pushed going to the park, and I'm grateful I haven't had to fight with her again.

There's a soft rap at my bedroom door while I'm pulling on my slacks.

"Who is it?"

"It's me, Paige." Her voice is soft, tentative.

"Just a second," I call back as I zip up my trousers and then stalk toward the door. I'll grab my shirt in a minute. I yank the door open, wondering what she's coming to my bedroom door for.

Is something wrong with Nova?

"Is everything okay?" I ask, glancing her up and down. I'm expecting to find my daughter at her side, but she's not there.

It's still early. She's probably in the playroom or getting dressed for the day. However, Paige helps with that task.

"The therapy appointment is this morning," she says.

I stare at her blankly. Why is she coming to my door to tell me what I already know? Did she think I forgot? "Yes, I know."

"If I'm coming with you, it might be good for me to know what I'm supposed to say. Are we married? Am I her mother and her nanny?"

I groan and throw my arms into the air. The whole point was that I didn't want to talk about any of it or think about it.

I leave the bedroom door open for her to follow me into the room while I grab a dress shirt from my closet.

"Shut the door, will you?" I glance back over my shoulder at her.

I don't need Dante or Nikki getting wind of this conversation.

The clasp of the door clicks into place. I breathe a sigh of relief and continue. "You will be accompanying me as her mother. Listen, I don't want to talk about Serene. If you show up and just go along with whatever I say, everything will be fine."

"Will it?" Paige asks. "From what I hear, Nova used to speak."

Pulling my shirt on, I spin around to face her. "Who told you that?" Anger stirs inside of me, and I step closer toward Paige, forgetting about the buttons on my shirt.

She doesn't back down or cower. Paige stands her ground. "Does it matter?"

"It was Ariella, wasn't it? That little brat!"

Paige doesn't flinch. "Who cares how I found out? The fact you're not denying it says more about your character than hers."

I should hate her for the way she's speaking to me, with such little respect, but instead, all I feel is his warmth mixed with anger. "You don't know what you're talking about."

"I heard Nova humming a lullaby the other day."

"You're lying." I don't believe her. It's all games and manipulation tactics to make me trust her and confide in her. Well, it's not going to work. I turn away, not meeting her stare while I button my shirt.

"I know you want what's best for your daughter. While I don't think lying to the therapist is the best option, I'm willing to do whatever you, as my employer, require."

"Good." I grab a tie from my rack in the closet. "I'm glad that's settled. You're dismissed."

I don't care whether Paige is done or not. I'm done with her for the moment. I want a few minutes of quiet before I have to endure pure torture at the hands of a shrink.

I'm probably overly dramatic. The therapist is for Nova, and she's not going to analyze my family.

At least I hope she's not going to look too deep into our lives. I wait for Paige to be gone, and the door closes behind her before I step toward my nightstand.

I pull open the top drawer and retrieve a small wooden box engraved with Serene's initials. It was a gift that I'd gotten for her on my travels overseas.

It was to hold her pictures, trinkets, mementos, anything she saw fit.

Lifting the lid, I see there are a handful of photographs, a movie stub ticket, and Nova's baby bracelet. I finger through the contents, searching out Serene's wedding band and engagement ring. The rings were fused, and after her death, I placed the contents in the wooden box.

Every so often, I glance in as a bitter reminder of all that I've lost.

Sometimes it brings me peace.

Usually, it brings me down to my knees with gut-wrenching sorrow but never any tears.

I don't see the ring at first glance. I dump the contents onto the bed.

Four photographs.

One ticket stub.

Nova's baby bracelet.

There's no wedding ring.

I swallow the lump in my throat. My eyes burn, and I storm out of the bedroom.

Dante and Nikki would never betray me. My men know better than to enter my room, let alone steal from me.

"Paige!" I scream out her name, demanding her to come to me.

17

PAIGE

Just as I finish getting Nova into her romper, Moreno is screaming my name at the top of his lungs.

What now?

He sounds pissed, and it sends a shudder through my body.

Nova's eyes are wide and her body tenses. "It'll be okay," I say and offer the little one a warm smile.

His footfalls are heavy as he stomps into my bedroom. I can hear the door open and wonder if he's ripped it right off its hinges.

Moreno barrels into Nova's room through the adjoining door.

"Care to explain why my late wife's wedding ring is missing?"

It's not a question.

I feel the accusation posed at me.

He steps closer, a little too close, as he's invading my personal space.

"I don't—" I start and cast a glance at Nova.

She's trembling and her eyes are filled with tears as they are sliding down her cheeks. Nova attempts not to move, frozen in place, but the fear radiating through her is visible.

Although, Moreno pays her no attention.

His anger, which seems to have turned to hatred, is burning at me like an inferno. He's about to erupt, and so I let him.

Anything to protect that little girl.

"I'm sorry. I shouldn't have taken the ring." I never touched his dead wife's ring, but he's dead set on believing I'm the villain.

"We don't have time right now. Downstairs. Now," he snaps.

I usher Nova out of the bedroom and down to the foyer to get ready to head out.

"I expect the ring back in the box as soon as we return home."

If Nova didn't take the ring, I'm royally screwed.

Does the little girl have sticky fingers?

Is there a chance one of the guards or someone who came in to clean the place saw it and pawned it?

"Am I still coming with you to the appointment?"

"Don't think you're getting out of it that easily," Moreno says. His top lip snarls. He's trying to control his anger.

Has he finally recognized how afraid Nova is of him?

"I wouldn't dream of it," I say.

We head outside, and I open the back door of his SUV, helping Nova into her car seat. I buckle her in nice and tight before climbing into the front seat.

Truthfully, I'd rather sit in the back with her. It feels safer.

Moreno slams on the gas. We hurry away from the cabin as the gates are opened for us to leave. How many more times will I be able to walk freely outside of the confines of the property?

———

Together, we sit in the waiting room. Nova is situated beside me on a double chair and Moreno is seated by himself.

Does it bother him that his daughter has chosen to sit with me instead of him?

Maybe he doesn't even notice, and I'm making more out of it than I should.

His jaw is tight, his hands clenched at his sides. He's still fuming about the ring he accused me of stealing.

I didn't take it. I didn't even know where it was to steal from him. But I have the sneaking suspicion that Nova knew where it was and she swiped it.

Call it intuition.

It could also be that she seems guilty, unable to so much as cast a glance at her father and is cuddling me at every opportunity that she gets.

The office door squeaks open. "Hi, Nova," the woman says. She bends down to Nova's level to introduce herself. "I'm Ellie. I see you brought a friend today. I have some crayons to color with in my office. Would you like to come see?"

Nova doesn't budge from the seat beside me as she clutches her stuffed giraffe tight.

"Nova, let's go," Moreno says. He doesn't offer even a hint of a smile. It's like he's waiting for her to obey him. Maybe that works on the guards, but Nova is a child.

I stand and offer her my hand. "Come on. It's okay." I give her a warm smile, wanting her not to be scared about the strange and unfamiliar place. "I know you like to draw, and I'll bet she has all the best colors."

She stares at me, eyes wide, and grips my hand.

"I'll be with you the entire time. So, will your daddy," I say. I'm not sure that assures her or not, but she climbs down from the chair and clutches my hand tight as we step into the therapist's office.

Moreno is right on our heels. I'd expect nothing less.

"Let me do the talking," he whispers into my ear as we take a seat on the sofa, the three of us.

Nova climbs between us.

I'm okay with that. It means I don't have to sit next to Moreno and right now, I don't want to cooperate with him.

I'd just assume I blow up his story, let the woman know every detail about Serene.

Wouldn't that help Nova?

Honestly, I'm not sure if it would help or make things worse for her. I can live with myself if I piss my boss off, but I can't handle hurting Nova. She doesn't deserve that type of treatment.

On a small table, are several blank sheets of paper and crayons. She glances at the crayons on the table but doesn't move from the sofa.

"How about we color together?" I say.

Scooting from the sofa, I glance over my shoulder at Nova and give her a warm smile and nod.

She's chewing her bottom lip. She wants to color, but she seems timid and afraid. I'm not sure of what—her father, the situation, something else?

I reach for the purple crayon, her favorite color, and start coloring quietly at the table.

Moreno begins speaking with Ellie, explaining some basic information, and Nova slips off the sofa and grabs the crayon from my hand.

She may not be great with sharing, but at least the kid knows what she wants.

I let her have the purple crayon, and she grabs a blank piece of paper and begins to scribble a drawing.

While I have no idea what she's visualizing, it's apparent that she's attentive, and her mind is no longer on the situation.

Quietly, I sneak back to the sofa and sit beside Moreno.

"And you two are happily married?" Ellie asks. "I only ask because sometimes fighting in the home can lead to—"

Moreno cuts her off. He wraps an arm around my shoulders, pulling me closer as he scoots toward me. "Yes, everything at home is wonderful. Isn't it?"

"She's been mute for as long as I can remember," I say. It's not a lie, not even in the least bit.

I glance down at my hand on my lap and realize we didn't come into this particularly planned. I'm not wearing a wedding band.

Is that why Moreno had been fuming earlier about Serene's ring? Had he intended for me to wear it to the appointment?

No.

That wasn't possible. Not with his outburst earlier at the house.

"Have there been any sudden changes in Nova's behavior or at home?" Ellie asks. She's got a pad of paper out, and she's scribbling down notes as we speak.

Ellie's situated across from us, but only a few feet away. Our conversation isn't hushed, but Nova doesn't seem to notice or care about us being in the room anymore.

"Nothing," Moreno says.

It's a lie. Can Ellie see through his charade?

"I want to help Nova, but the more you tell me, the better I can be equipped to determine what might be going on with your daughter," Ellie says. "Anything either of you tells me will be kept in the strictest of confidence."

"There's nothing to tell," Moreno says.

Ellie nods and puts her notes away. "Do you mind if I talk to Nova?" she asks.

"Have at it," Moreno says and gestures for Ellie to approach Nova.

Ellie is soft-spoken and steps out from the chair, kneeling at the table. She grabs a pink crayon and a piece of paper.

"I like your picture," Ellie says.

Nova glances up at the woman before averting her eyes back down to the drawing. There's a faint smile quirking at the corner of Nova's lips like she's trying not to grin at the compliment.

I see it.

Does Ellie see it?

What about Moreno?

———

"Six hundred dollars an hour for that?"

"Technically, it was an hour and a half," I offer as we head back out to the car. I'm buckling Nova into her car seat. "And the first appointment is always more money."

He shoots me a look. "How would you know?"

"What? Do you think I've never seen a therapist before? My life isn't rainbows and butterflies."

He snorts under his breath. "Could have fooled me."

I roll my eyes and shut the back door after Nova is secure in her seat. Yanking open the passenger side, I plop into the seat and give him a hard stare. "You should watch what you say."

His brow furrows.

I don't give a shit what he says about me. What bothers me is the way he speaks about Nova in front of her. The kid already has issues, and to pretend they don't exist and then further amplify them is just plain cruel.

I slam the door shut and buckle my seatbelt while he puts the car in drive and hightails us out of Spring Valley.

I don't know whether there aren't any child therapists in Breckenridge or if he prefers to drive farther from town so that no one would know his business.

The drive is silent, and I glance behind me at Nova. She's preoccupied with her giraffe. Her lips are moving, but she isn't saying anything aloud.

The moment she realizes I'm watching her, she shuts her lips.

Yeah, that's what I thought.

Nova is hiding something.

As far as I'm concerned, so is Moreno.

The whole fricking Ricci family is drowning in secrets.

I don't want to drown too.

I want to be set free, but I feel like I know too much, and he'll never let me go.

18

MORENO

She stole my dead wife's ring.

I can't let it go. The fact she confessed is even worse.

I thought maybe something happened to it, and I was overreacting, but I know I returned the ring to its rightful place the last time I held Serene's wedding ring.

The nice guy act is over.

Now that we're done pretending to be married for the therapy appointment, I can return to feeling angry and hurt that she'd betray me.

Maybe I should fire her for stealing from me.

I've killed men for less, but she's good with Nova, and I can't let that be forgotten.

It's the only reason I'm not sending her down to the dungeon to sleep. She's good with my kid.

Shit.

My cock twitches in my trousers.

I do not want to feel anything toward the little thief. But my body betrays me, along with my heart.

"Get out of the car," I grit between clenched teeth.

I shut off the engine and climb out in haste.

The nanny is out of the vehicle before I can open the back door to retrieve my daughter. She's already unbuckling her like a pro.

"I can do that," I say. Anger boils in my blood, and I want her nowhere near my kin.

A frown is etched on her face. Did she forget that she stole from me? "Did I say something wrong?"

"You stole my dead wife's ring." I yank open the back door to grab Nova, and she throws her arms up to Paige, wanting the nanny over her father.

Fuck.

I didn't intend to scare Nova.

I forget how easily she frightens.

Nova clutches onto Paige, burying her face in the nanny's neck.

Paige is gentle and kind, warm and compassionate. She rubs at Nova's back as she carries her into the house.

I don't understand how someone who can be so caring can also be so callous to steal from me.

"Do I not pay you enough? Is that the problem?" I'm chasing after her, demanding an answer.

I held my tongue long enough on the drive home. I can't be kept silent any longer. The betrayal cuts into me like a dagger to the heart from behind.

"I trusted you," I seethe.

Paige doesn't answer me. She carries Nova to the playroom down the hallway.

"We can have this conversation later," she says to me over her shoulder.

I don't do later. I want to fight now. She owes me an explanation.

"We're having it now." I refuse to back down. I don't let anyone walk all over me, and I feel like I've let Paige do that by stealing from me.

She gently sets Nova down in the playroom and stalks out into the hallway. "Are you going to fire me?"

"I ought to do more than just fire you."

She shakes her head, clearly not understanding the implication.

You betray the Ricci family. You die. It's as simple as that. But she's not mafia. She's the nanny. And I can't forget how good she is with Nova. I hate their connection.

Jealousy seeps into my veins.

"Dock my pay," Paige says. "Whatever the ring cost, I'll pay you back."

Does she not realize the sentimental value of the treasure? "It's not about the money. My wife is dead. Murdered. I can't replace the ring. Just like I can't replace her. Until the ring is returned to me, you're forbidden from leaving."

"What?" Her eyes widen. "You can't do that, sir."

I just did.

She'll learn to respect me and my authority.

"You heard me," I say and step closer, staring down at her.

She takes several small steps backward, her heels hitting the edge of the wall. There's nowhere else for her to go.

I have her trapped.

The heat radiates off her body. The hallway feels warm, stuffy, and suffocating. I'm tired of her games and antics. Why can't she just hand over the ring?

Did she throw it out?

Flush it down the toilet?

Does she hate me that much?

I can't fathom what kind of person would steal from the mafia. Then again, she probably doesn't realize we're that type of family.

Her eyes are wide and bright. Her hands tremble at her sides.

I pretend not to notice the fear as I trap her. My hand comes up against the wall, not letting her slip away, even if she wanted to escape.

She hasn't tried to run or flee.

I can't fathom why.

"If you want your freedom, you'll return my dead wife's ring you stole."

Her eyelid twitches for a brief second. There's something behind her gaze that I don't recognize.

Is it anger? Resentment?

"Do you smell that?" Paige asks.

That is not the response I was expecting.

"What? Is this a game to you?" My voice echoes down the corridor.

The smell wafts from the playroom and burns my nostrils.

Smoke.

19

PAIGE

Just as my grumpy boss reams me for stealing, something I didn't do, I smell smoke.

When he finally realizes I'm not trying to play him to get away, we rush into the playroom just a few feet away from us.

The curtains are ablaze.

Nova stands near the fire, frozen. The flames lap all around her as she's coughing because of the smoke.

"Nova!" I shriek.

Thick smoke curls around the room as the fire quickly spreads from one surface to the next. The toys are wood and paper, highly flammable.

Fire rolls up the walls and to the ceiling.

"I'll get Nova. Grab a fire extinguisher!" I shout at Moreno. The longer we wait, the less likely the fire will remain contained.

I rush into the playroom, coughing on the thick smoke as I grab the little girl and carry her out of the playroom.

The smoke detector signals and emits a high-frequency pitch. It's tied to every smoke detector within the premises, and they all go off.

Moreno hurries back with a fire extinguisher, dousing the flames, but it isn't enough.

Two more guards, now aware of the imminent threat, bring additional fire extinguishers from other parts of the home, using the canisters to smother the blaze.

Dante is behind them with one more fire extinguisher, and Nikki is ushering Luca down the stairs toward the front door. "Should I call 9-1-1?" Nikki asks her hand on her phone.

"No, we've got it smothered," Moreno says.

The fire is out, but smoke still wafts through the playroom and has extended beyond the hallway.

"Open the windows and someone shut off that damned alarm!" Moreno shouts.

"What the hell happened?" Dante glances from Moreno to me. Like I had something to do with it.

Nova's arms are wrapped snug around my neck, and I shift her to my hip. Her fingers fumble with something. I don't quite know what it is when it drops to the ground with a clunk.

A lighter.

"Where the hell did she get a lighter?" Moreno bends down and snatches the disposable lighter from the floor.

Shit.

Nova did this?

I'm sure it was an accident.

She couldn't have known what she was doing and the damage and danger that she caused.

"Did you give this to her?" Moreno stares at me, showing me the lighter.

"Of course not!"

How could he think that I would give a four-year-old a lighter? Is he going to accuse me of giving her matches or telling her to stick a fork in an electric socket next?

"I'm sorry," Luca's soft and fragile voice carries from the door. His bottom lip trembles.

"Son, where did you get the lighter?" Dante asks a little too calmly as he approaches Luca, bending down to his level.

I swallow nervously. While I had nothing to do with it, I'm scared the kid might lie and throw me to the wolves.

"One of the kids brought it to camp," Luca says. "I hid it in the playroom. I didn't know Nova would find it."

"We'll talk about this later," Dante says. "Open the windows. We need to clear out the smoke."

Dante turns his attention toward Moreno. "Why wasn't the nanny watching your daughter?"

Moreno's lips pinch together. "We were having a discussion and let Nova play alone in the playroom. We didn't expect her to stumble onto a lighter."

He's defending his daughter.

Good.

Dante gives a sharp nod. "It's a relief no one was hurt. I want a word with you, Moreno."

"Of course, boss. Paige, take Nova outside for some fresh air into the garden. Go through the kitchen."

I don't need an escort, and I'm pleased that Moreno lets me accompany Nova alone out to the garden.

The fresh air is welcome, and the moment we're outside, Nova wiggles to get down from my grasp.

I put her feet down on the brick patio and take a seat on the wooden bench. The garden is small, intimate, and has an assortment of vegetables sprouting.

Nova leans forward and points to the sugar snap peas flowering. A few are ready to be picked. I twist them off, one by one, and hand them to Nova.

She pops one in her mouth and chomps loudly, happily distracted.

The fear from the fire seems to be gone for now.

Will she have nightmares tonight or in the future because of the fire?

I reach for Nova and pull her onto my lap for a little talk. "Did you take your mama's ring from your daddy's bedroom?"

While I haven't seen the ring, I suspect she's harboring some guilt over it.

Her eyes fall to the ground, and she wiggles again to get away from me.

"I'm not mad," I say in a soft and soothing voice. Scaring her isn't going to help. Neither is berating her.

"Your daddy is sad that the ring is gone. He misses your mom very much. I'll bet you miss her too."

Nova slowly glances up at me with bright eyes and gives a brief nod.

"Do you know where the ring is?" I ask.

Her lips are pressed tight together.

Moreno will never let me leave.

20

MORENO

Wordlessly, she carries Nova down the hallway, farther into the house for the garden outside. I don't want them wandering away from the property, and I can't be too cautious with the DeLucas out there, still hunting down my family.

Nikki and Luca head out the front door, with Leone escorting them out for the afternoon.

The guards continue to open windows to clear out the remainder of the smoke. We head into the library and do the same, opening the window, which peeks out into the garden.

I catch a glimpse of Nova and Paige sitting on a bench together.

"You're back for five minutes and the place practically is up in flames," Dante says.

"What can I say? I'm irresistible."

Dante gives a loud snort. "Keep it in your pants. I don't need you burning down the compound from the heat you two give off."

I roll my eyes. "Funny. Nothing's happening between us." Doesn't he realize that?

Of course, how could he? He doesn't know Paige stole from me.

Do I tell him?

If I do, he's going to expect retribution. I don't blame him. He's don. No one steals from our family, ever.

If I don't, then I'm protecting her, and why should I do that? She betrayed me. I owe her nothing.

"Right," Dante says and quirks a sideways grin. "Nothing so hot that you didn't notice Nova playing with the lighter and starting a fire?"

"We were having a disagreement," I say.

It's not a lie.

Dante snorts under his breath. "Ordinarily, I'd tell you to get laid, fuck the nanny, and get rid of the sexual tension, but shit. If your kid is starting fires to get your attention, maybe you need to keep it in your pants, Moreno."

That wasn't what happened.

But I saw his point.

"It won't happen again."

Paige should have been watching Nova, and she wasn't because I'd cornered her in the hallway. I didn't want to admit that having her pressed up against the wall made my cock twitch in my pants.

She had that effect on me.

Why?

"I think you should fuck her," Dante says.

"You're not serious." He may have liked to play the field before settling down with Nikki, but that wasn't me.

Dante doesn't so much as smile. "I'm dead serious. Your wife is gone, and you deserve to be happy. She seems to be good with Nova, and it's clear you have the hots for her."

"I don't."

"Liar," Dante says.

"Shut up." There aren't too many people who can get away with talking to their boss like that. "I can't believe you're encouraging me to fuck her."

He laughs under his breath. "I'd take you to the bar as your wingman, but I don't see you picking up a girl for sex. That's not your style. The nanny, though, she's hot. It's a good thing I'm already taken. Unless, of course, she's interested in threesomes. I could ask Nikki—"

"Don't you dare!"

A grin cracks across his face.

He knows just what to say to get to me, and it worked.

"It wouldn't bother you if you didn't find her attractive."

That was never the problem. Paige is very attractive. Countless times, I've mentally undressed her and imagined driving my cock inside her warmth.

"Attraction isn't the issue. She's my daughter's nanny."

Dante shrugs. "Where's the problem? If it doesn't work out, she'll quit. Paige isn't going to stick around after you stick it to her. So, you'll have to find new help, but in the meantime, you can move on and maybe not be so damned grumpy all the time."

"I'm not grumpy."

"Right, and the sun doesn't rise every damn day. You're Oscar the Grouch. Just ask Nova."

My eyes twitch.

Nova doesn't speak. At least not anymore.

He knows that.

But she used to speak all the time, and he's not ignorant of the fact that she's clammed up since her mother died.

Serene isn't the only one who died that day.

Nova's nanny was murdered, too. I can't help but wonder if Nova witnessed it, and that's why she's become mute.

21

PAIGE

Nova and I spend most of the afternoon in the garden. It would be easy to climb the small white fence, but how far would we get? The perimeter is guarded.

While Moreno threatened that I couldn't leave the premises until the ring was returned, I haven't tried to leave yet.

It has only been a few hours.

But the suffocating feeling of being held against my will is enough to make me antsy.

I need out.

Nova is my priority during the day, though, and while she is awake, I won't let her out of my sight. Especially after the fire.

We play outside for several hours. Leone brings us lunch while workers are being shuffled in and out of the house, making repairs to the playroom.

Thankfully, there wasn't any structural damage, according to Leone. As dinner nears, we are brought inside to eat in the kitchen.

I haven't spoken with Moreno, let alone seen him. He hasn't so much as acknowledged Nova's or my existence.

Is he angry that Nova stared the fire? She couldn't have known what she was doing was dangerous.

The lighter hadn't taken much to trigger the flame, just a flip of the lid back. No safety. No child-proof lock.

It was a disaster waiting to happen.

Who the hell brought it to a children's camp? Had it been another kid?

There isn't much I can do. Luca isn't my responsibility, and I'm confident that Dante and Nikki will handle the situation.

After dinner, Rhys ushers us upstairs, ensuring we are kept away from the playroom while the repairs continue.

The lock clicks into place the moment the door is shut behind us.

"Seriously?" I mutter.

Why is Moreno having us locked in our room?

What if there is another fire?

Is he worried that I'm going to try to escape, or about the workers downstairs?

"How about we get you cleaned up in a nice warm bath and then read a story before bed?"

Nova scrunches her nose. She doesn't like my suggestion. I'm guessing it's the part involving going to bed. I don't know any child who enjoys bedtime.

As an adult, I look forward to crashing for the night.

"Come on. I'll let you pick out two books tonight."

The smile widens on her face as she follows me into her bathroom.

There's already a fresh towel laid out, and I draw her bath water while she strips down for me without any help.

Bathing her is a priority. I didn't realize how much her clothes reek of smoke, but as I grab them to throw in the hamper, I get an extra whiff and clear my throat, trying not to cough.

My throat feels parched and raspy.

She plays with her rubber ducky in the bath while I wash her hair and get her nice and squeaky clean.

I still want to find the ring that she swiped before she forgets where she hid it.

She finishes in her bath, and I dry her off and help her get into her pajamas. "Do you remember the ring you borrowed from your daddy?" I ask.

I don't want to accuse her of stealing, but she looked extremely guilty earlier when it had been brought up.

She purses her lips together but doesn't answer verbally.

Not that I expect her to tell me where it is.

But she turns her head and her eyes glance at her stuffed giraffe. She pokes at the butt of the giraffe, tapping it and pulling the flap down. There is a secret compartment in her toy.

Nova reveals the sparkling diamond ring.

I hold out my hand for her to place it in my palm.

She's tentative at first before she deposits the ring into my hand and wordlessly climbs beneath the covers on the bed.

"Thank you." I kiss her cheek and place the ring on my finger so that I don't lose it. I'd never forgive myself if something were to happen to the band, and I know that Moreno wouldn't either.

I read her two bedtime stories as promised before tucking her in and slipping out of her bedroom. I close the adjoining door most of the way. If she needs me, I hope that she'll come find me during the night.

Until now, she's been a sound sleeper, but after the fire today, I can't help but worry about her.

I shower, cleansing myself from the smell of smoke that permeates my skin. I can smell it on my dirty clothes and shove the linens into the hamper.

I slip on an oversized t-shirt and panties and climb under the covers with my eReader. I'm tired, and I'm not sure that I can read even a few pages, but I'm not ready to go to sleep yet.

The sun is still out.

It sets late in the summer, and while the bedroom curtains help, there's still light peeking through the shades.

My phone buzzes with a text on the bedside table.

I reach for the device. There aren't too many people who have my number.

Hey, it's Ariella. How's the big, grumpy bosshole?

I smile and can't help but laugh. I never told her he was grumpy or a bosshole, but it's like she can read my mind. She did know Nova before her mother passed away, so maybe he's always been this difficult to deal with. I had assumed it was because his wife died, but I didn't know him before her passing.

He's a handful.

I'll bet. Do you want to come over this weekend for a girls' day? I have wine.

That sounds perfect, but would Moreno give me the day off?

Not sure I can escape, but I'll try.

Escape? What, are you captive?

I start to type *yes* but then quickly delete it. I don't need her calling the police and making more of a mess of my situation.

Very funny. I'll let you know if I can get away.

Okay. Enjoy your Friday night!

I laugh under my breath. Yeah, I'm enjoying my Friday locked in my bedroom with a four-year-old in the next room over.

She texts me her address, just in case. Dropping the phone back on the bedside table, I dive into my book.

Not two minutes into my story, the adjoining door squeaks open.

"Nova?" I glance at the door to find Moreno standing there, staring at me again.

Is he planning on making it a habit to come into my bedroom unannounced?

I place my tablet down on the bed and stare up at him.

He's wearing jeans and a black t-shirt. His hair is ruffled a bit. It looks like he was helping with the repairs in the playroom. There's dried paint on his jeans and a smudge on his arm and cheek.

"Nova went down for bed without any trouble." I can only imagine that he's come into my room to talk about his daughter.

After the day we had, I don't blame him for wanting to check in on her, especially since he seemed non-existent for the afternoon.

"That's good. And I saw you bathed her." He takes a seat at the edge of my bed.

"Yeah, we both kind of stunk after the fire," I say.

Moreno smells good, even with sweat, dirt, and smoke lingering on his skin. He probably shouldn't be sitting on my bed right now, or at all, but I don't care.

I like his attention and his company. I try not to stare for too long before I avert my gaze.

"Listen, I was wondering if I could have tomorrow off. I'd like to go—"

"No." Moreno's answer is short and curt. "I told you, you're not going anywhere."

I slide the ring off my finger and hand the diamond band to Moreno. "I found your wife's ring."

He laughs darkly and shakes his head. "I hoped that I was wrong about you. About this," he says, snatching the small piece of jewelry from my palm. "But apparently, I wasn't."

Moreno stands. "I'm disappointed in you."

"I'm not your daughter or some kid you can boss around."

"No, you're my employee, my child's nanny," he says with such disgust that it roils my stomach.

Does he think that he's better than me? He certainly acts like it with his nose held up and that smug grin plastered on his face.

I want to wipe it off. Prove to him that I'm more than just some nanny.

He heads for the adjoining door. Even if he wanted to escape from my bedroom door, I don't imagine that he can. It's probably still locked from the outside by the guards.

"I'm a better nanny to your daughter than you are a father," I mutter on his way out.

Moreno stops dead in his tracks.

Shit.

He heard me.

22

MORENO

It's not bad enough that Paige dares to steal from me and then wear Serene's ring on her finger like she's my bride, but then to go and say she's a better parent to my daughter than I am?

The nerve of her!

Well, technically, she didn't use the word parent, but it's the same difference.

I can't let it go.

I should walk out. Leave her alone and bury myself in work.

Even sleep would be a welcoming distraction.

But my feet lead me back around. Maybe it's my heart interfering. My head is certainly in the right place, screaming for me to get out before I do something I will regret.

"Excuse me?" I take two strides. My footsteps aren't soft and quiet.

I hope I don't wake Nova from slumber, but I can't be any quieter than I already am. This is me keeping it down.

My voice booms as I snarl at Paige.

Her eyes widen, and she snaps her lips shut.

Yeah, she didn't think I heard her. Well, I did. "Care to say that again to my face?"

It's a challenge.

She presses her lips together, rolling them between her teeth.

My gaze lingers longer than it should on her lips, but she doesn't say anything if she notices.

"I will be taking tomorrow off," Paige says.

Goodness, does the girl have no understanding of not leaving the compound? "You're not leaving until I allow it."

"Excuse me?" she huffs and sits up in bed, pushing her legs over the edge. "I'm not some girl you can hole up and keep captive."

Does she realize I'm keeping her here to protect her?

Vance will come after her. And when he finds her, he'll torture her, rape her, and kill her. It's a game to see what he can do to destroy my family and how long we survive.

She doesn't get it.

How could she? I haven't exactly been open and honest with her about Serene's death or Laura, our last nanny.

"Do you honestly believe that I'm keeping you here for my pleasure?" I laugh at the absurdity of her suggestion. "You're Nova's nanny, and I have somewhere to be tomorrow. Which means you will be here, watching my daughter."

Her brow furrows.

The cogs must be going in her head.

"Then you won't have a problem if I take her with me for the day out?"

I toss my hands into the air. "You seriously can't listen? You are not leaving. Nova is not leaving. If you so much as step foot outside, I'll have the guards detain you and sequester you to your room for the next month," I seethe.

She is trying my patience.

"We can't go anywhere?" Paige asks. Her jaw is practically on the floor.

"I will let you know when you can go for an outing, and you will be required to bring one of the guards with you."

"Great, a spy," she says under her breath.

She's not wrong. Leone has been informed to report anything of importance, and after she met with Ariella, I don't intend to tell him to stop. "You ought to watch your tone and your tongue."

Paige strikes me as a girl who probably got into a lot of trouble in her teenage years, testing the boundaries, pushing her parents to their breaking point.

I can only hope that Nova won't be like that when she gets older. Then again, with Paige as her nanny, is it inevitable?

"Are you done?" Paige asks, reaching for her eReader. "I'd like to get back to my book."

"I'll tell you when we're done." I step closer, grabbing her tablet and tossing it farther onto the queen-sized bed, out of her reach.

She opens her mouth to object. A frown crosses her features when I lean in and steal a kiss along with her breath.

I've never known Paige to be silent, ever.

Maybe I should take Dante's advice and let my guard down and give in to temptation. She's fiery, and the tension between us sizzles in the air.

While I loved Serene, the energy between us was never anywhere this charged. The temptation is impossible to ignore, especially the moan she emits from the back of her throat while we kiss.

Damn.

She knows how to make me powerless.

One kiss, and I'm willing to give her anything.

Even her freedom.

But I can't give in.

I won't.

Her safety is my priority, and if I allow her to leave, she may never see another sunrise. I pull back from the kiss, my lips tingle, and my heart pounds wildly against my ribcage.

Paige leans in for another kiss.

But I pull back to stop her.

23

PAIGE

Two minutes ago, we were arguing about him not letting me leave, let alone take Nova off the property, and then he decided to kiss me.

I should be angry with him, but the kiss tore down my defenses.

I want more.

My fingers fist his shirt, pulling him down on top of me as I desire another searing hot kiss with my boss.

That small nagging voice in my head reminds me that he's a bad boy.

Trouble.

The worst choice I could go for—the biggest mistake of my life.

There's only one way to silence that voice.

And that's with another kiss.

The bedsheets are bunched between us as we kiss, and I lift my hips long enough to push the sheets down with my knees. I'm hot and sweaty between his kisses and the blankets, and it's just too much.

But I don't want to push Moreno away.

I want more of him.

I want more with him.

While I know that I should stop, I can't. My fingers slide beneath his black t-shirt, and I run my palms against his skin.

One kiss leads to two.

We're tangled together, the bedsheets between my legs as he pins my arms above my head with one hand.

His fingers skim over my stomach, the pads of his fingers soft and teasing as they dance over my t-shirt.

I feel partially naked with only a t-shirt and panties on, but I don't care.

Will he be surprised and pleased to discover the purple lace thong? I wore it for him.

Not that I ever thought he'd see it on me, but I slipped it on, excited with the fantasy that he might.

"What do you want?" Moreno asks, staring down at me.

He still has my arms trapped against the mattress, pinned above my head.

My chest rises and falls with every gasp of air and breath that I take.

"You," I whisper up at him, already panting.

The last thing I want is for him to stop or pull away and leave things unfinished between us.

Moreno leans down for another fiery kiss, his tongue pushing past my lips and inside my mouth.

He knows how to kiss a woman, really kiss her.

Thankfully, I'm already lying in bed, or I'd be falling to the ground, weak at the knees.

My back arches off the mattress as we kiss. I want to feel him pressed tightly against me. I crave his touch.

I wrap my legs around him, pulling him down to me as I moan.

His weight crushes me in the best possible way, making me feel safe.

Moreno grunts and then pulls back, his hands releasing his hold on me as he lets go and climbs off the bed.

I don't know what happened. Did I do something wrong? "Moreno?"

"Don't," he snaps. "You can't use sex to fix what you did." He adjusts his pants and dusts off his shirt, like that will erase the last few minutes and the feelings along with it.

"I'm not using—"

"I don't want to hear it," Moreno says. "You stole Serene's ring." He huffs on his way back through the adjoining door and out of Nova's bedroom.

"Fuck," I groan under my breath and grab the pillow beside me, covering my face with it as I scream with frustration.

———

Moreno has a way of avoiding me.

After what happened in my bedroom over a week ago, I haven't seen him for more than a brief minute or two.

He's doing everything he can to stay away from me.

And usually, that would be okay. It's not like I've ever wanted to hang around my boss before. But Moreno isn't just any boss.

Being in his presence brings butterflies to my stomach. However, I'm not sure if that's fear-driven or desire.

It could be both.

No doubt he's a powerful man, and that level of confidence and control that he yields, I find exhilarating. He's unlike anyone I've ever known.

Will I ever get to know any more about him?

Nikki might spill a few details if I can corner her, but I want to hear it from him.

I want to talk to him. I feel like I need to explain about Serene's ring, except I can't without betraying Nova.

Hasn't the girl been through enough already?

The door to Nova's bedroom squeaks open, and I know that Moreno checks on his daughter every night, but he doesn't come to my room any longer.

It's probably for the best.

At least that's what I tell myself. But I'm not happy about his decision. I want to get to know him.

For some crazy reason, I like being around him. I'm honestly not sure why. What we have is far from love. It's attraction. Desire. Lust. Maybe chemistry. I'm not convinced it's anything more than physical.

And while I wouldn't normally throw myself in a relationship with a man I'm working for and living with, I can't stop myself, either.

Seeking him out is like a thrill ride at the amusement park.

I crave a glance from him, a long, hard stare.

It would also be nice if he didn't hate me in the process.

It's late, and Nova is sound asleep.

I wait for Moreno to check on her in bed before I corner him, quietly sneaking out of bed and stepping into Nova's room.

Moreno doesn't so much as look up at me. He feels my presence, though. Or maybe he heard me enter. I tried to be quiet, but the floorboards squeak.

"Go back to bed," he whispers harshly toward me.

I don't listen to him.

Moreno points at the open bedroom door for me to return to my room.

He may want me to listen to him, but I have no intention of returning to my bedroom alone. Instead, I fold my arms across my chest.

Considering how stubborn he's been all week, it's my turn.

Nova's bedroom is dark, except for the nightlight.

He looks exhausted and worn. Is it work keeping him preoccupied or something else?

Me?

No, I don't wield much power.

When I don't relent, he finally gives in and gestures for me to follow him into my bedroom.

Good. We can finally talk, get things out in the open. Maybe I can convince him to let me take Nova off the property for an afternoon.

He holds out his hand, and I step into my room and spin around, only to find the adjoining door snapped shut on my heel.

Bastard!

24

MORENO

I can't sleep. I'm not necessarily making it easy for anyone else in the house to sleep, either.

Nova, thankfully, is a sound sleeper.

But after slamming the door behind Paige, I need space and, more importantly, time.

Time to figure out what the hell I'm going to do.

"We're going out," Dante says as he steps out of his bedroom.

"What?" I can't remember the last time the two of us went out for fun and not business. Since he's been tied down to Nikki, the party going, sleep with any girl with a pulse has been tamed.

It's a rare sight to see and I'm happy for him.

Dante deserves Nikki. She certainly wasn't an easy catch.

He grabs me by the arm and leads me down the stairs, away from Nova's bedroom and, more importantly, Paige's room.

"It's clear you need a night out, away from whatever the two of you have going on." Dante is usually more direct.

I anticipate he'll ask me about Paige while we're out of the house, which is fine. I just don't want her listening to our conversation. Not that I've discovered her eavesdropping, I haven't. It's just the ring, the fact she stole it, that I can't let go of.

How could I?

But I can't confide in Dante, or he'll kick her ass to the curb.

Why do I want to protect her?

"What about Nikki?"

"I don't need her permission," Dante says and smirks. "She's out tonight with her friends."

I laugh under my breath. Is Dante's suggestion for us to go out for him or for me? "What about the kids?"

"The nanny is here, right?"

I give a weak nod.

"Don't make me order you to come out with me and have fun." Dante smacks me on the back and nudges me forward to follow him out the door.

He would do that to insist I join him tonight. "No orders needed, boss."

———

"You can't tell me none of the girls here are attractive," Dante says.

I swear he's trying to get me laid.

We're in the VIP lounge of the bar that he owns. It's a bit seedy for my taste. The bartender brings over a bottle of whiskey for Dante. They know his preference. It's one of the advantages of owning the establishment.

She brings two empty glasses with the bottle and a soda on the side for me. Why she ever brings an empty whiskey glass for me is baffling, but tonight, I might actually indulge in liquoring myself up.

Anything to avoid feeling—what, exactly?

The last time I was here was when I interviewed Paige.

Dante pours a glass of whiskey for himself, and I gesture for him to pour me one, too.

He always orders top-shelf.

"Who said this bottle was for you?" Dante laughs and pours me a drink. "She must be getting to you."

I grab the glass from the table and glance over at him. "Who?"

Dante grabs his own drink and clinks our glasses together as if we're toasting. "The new nanny. She is hot. I have to admit, if you hired her for her looks, I wouldn't blame you. She's got a fine ass when she walks. Hell, even Nikki thinks she's hot."

"She did not say that." I don't believe him.

He shrugs and sips his whiskey, not admitting whether what Nikki said was true or not.

He isn't wrong, though. Paige is every bit of a fantasy for me, and I hate myself for how she makes me feel. It'd be easier to be numb inside, like before I met her, after my wife's death.

"Are you going to tell me what happened between the two of you?" Dante asks, but I get the distinct feeling he isn't really asking. He's waiting for me to explain why all the tension and avoidance lately.

I've done everything that I can to not spend more than two minutes with Paige for the past week.

"Nothing."

"And the fire?" Dante asks, tilting his head, staring at me.

That has been on my mind, putting Nova first, and making sure that she's not getting into trouble.

"I'm sorry about the damage—"

Dante waves his hand dismissively. "We're past that, Moreno. Luca should never have brought home a lighter from camp, let alone left it in the playroom for Nova to discover. I'm asking about Paige."

He's always been direct with me. We both have, but this time I don't want to tell him about Paige.

When I take another sip of whiskey and grimace, he laughs and brings his glass to his lips.

"Wow. You'd rather drink than talk. Okay." He downs his glass of whiskey and pours a second drink for himself.

While I'd prefer to nurse my drink, it's either talk or shove something against my mouth so I don't have to speak, which means drinking whiskey.

I down the drink and refill the glass quickly.

Maybe it'll make my lips loose and sink the inevitable ship. It might as well be the fucking Titanic.

"Let me guess. You slept together, and she regrets it." Dante takes a stab at the cloud looming above me.

He's wrong.

Maybe I should let him believe that's why I'm pissed, but I didn't fuck her. Sure, we kissed. I wanted to wrestle her on the bed and show her what it's like to be consumed completely by one person, but it's nothing more than a fleeting fantasy.

"I haven't seen her naked."

Dante snorts.

"Doesn't mean you can't make her scream the big 'o' even with her clothes still on."

I roll my eyes at his crudeness. "She stole from me."

Fuck.

I wasn't going to tell him.

I swore to myself that the secret would stay between Paige and me. I reach for the whiskey bottle and pour myself a second glass.

Already, I'm spilling all my secrets, and I've barely had anything to drink.

Dante used to joke that I'm the worst mobster—one who hates liquor. It's not that I hate the taste or the effect it has on me.

The truth is that I hate what it did to my old man, how it made him into a monster. And I don't want to become that guy, the one who beats his woman and kid.

I swore I'd never become that, but here I am, having whiskey just like my old man.

I've avoided it all my life like the plague, but I know one night won't turn me into *him*. Though it still doesn't soften the blow as I refill my glass again and swallow the amber liquid as I spill my thoughts to Dante.

"I caught Paige wearing Serene's wedding ring."

Dante's mouth is hanging open.

I laugh darkly and finish my third glass of whiskey before pouring a fourth.

"I've rendered you speechless," I say.

Dante holds his glass in his hand and swirls the whiskey around for a beat. "There has to be more to the story."

He's not wrong. When is Dante ever wrong?

I don't want to confess that I went looking for the ring to have her wear to the therapy session. Dante doesn't know that Paige accompanied me, pretending to be Nova's mother.

When did I fuck up my life?

I give him the condensed version and stare back at him, waiting to hear what he has to say.

He's quiet. I've never known Dante to be silent.

Shit.

Did I render him speechless twice?

"I still think there's more to the story. Why would Paige go through your dresser and steal the ring?" Dante asks. "She had to know that she'd get caught."

"Why does anyone steal anything?" I throw my arms up into the air.

Dante ticks his fingers off with each answer that he gives. "Money. Attention. The thrill of getting caught."

I don't believe that's why Paige stole the ring. "No." I can't let go of the fact that she wore it when I saw her in bed.

"She could just be obsessed with you and wants to marry you."

I don't find his brand of humor the least bit funny right now.

"Do you want my suggestion or not?" Dante asks.

"I'd prefer to wallow in my misery." I pour another glass of whiskey, and Dante snatches the bottle, cutting me off from any more.

"You've had enough to drink, and I'm tired of watching you mope around. She's a beautiful woman, and while I don't take kindly to thieves, it's hard to fathom that she stole the ring to pawn when she was caught wearing it." He snaps his fingers as if an idea just hit him.

"What?" I'm not sure I'm ready to hear whatever it is he's about to suggest.

"Paige probably has a crush on you and went snooping. Maybe she stumbled onto the ring, slid it on to pretend to be married to you, and couldn't get it off?"

"You watch too much television," I mutter. There is no way that's what happened. That doesn't sound the least bit like something Paige would do.

Besides, she took it off and handed it to me. It didn't seem stuck. Although I don't really know Paige that well, anything is possible, I suppose.

"I've been credited with having an overactive imagination," Dante says, correcting me. "Nikki doesn't complain."

"How are things between you and Nikki?" I ask, steering the conversation away from my lack of a love life.

"Good. Never been better. The sex, I tell you, Moreno, it's dynamite." Dante's eyes light up, and the smile widens on his face.

He seems stoked to talk about Nikki and their sex life.

I want to drown myself behind the bar.

That's not to say that I'm not happy for him. I'm ecstatic. He was a miserable bastard before he met Nikki. Chasing any piece of ass he could land in his bed.

Nikki turned the deadliest and most cunning man into a father.

And he turned her into his wife.

A small pang of jealousy rips through me.

I want that.

The same level of commitment, undying affection, and desire. There's love between them, but it's the passion that's insurmountable.

Did I have that with Serene? I was madly in love with her, but we weren't perfect.

"You're quiet. Too quiet," Dante says.

"Maybe you're right, and it's time that I move on," I say.

Serene's been gone a year. Basking in sorrow and pity hasn't helped my daughter or me.

Dante glances around the bar. "There are a few girls at the bar. Do you want me to be your wingman?"

"They barely look old enough to drink." I'm not the least bit interested in dating a girl just out of college. "Not my type," I say, emphasizing my disinterest.

"I know. Your type is Paige, but she's your daughter's nanny and a thief, from what you tell me."

I really wish that I hadn't told him about the ring.

There isn't anyone in the bar who looks remotely like Paige. The girls all look young and are caked in makeup. I swear the bartender and bouncer need to be checking I.D.s better.

"I said it weeks ago, and I'll say it again. Just bang the nanny."

I cough, clearing my throat. Sometimes Dante still shocks me. It's not the first time that I've heard that suggestion from him, but I'm not going to fuck the nanny, no matter how much I want to sleep with her.

"Any other suggestions? What would Nikki suggest?"

"You expect me to know what my wife thinks?" Dante rolls his eyes and laughs. "We're betting on when you stick it to her."

I should be angry with Dante, but I'm not. It's rather amusing, considering we all live under the same roof. "That's why you want me to screw her? Did you bet that it'll happen on a certain date or something?"

"I bet Nikki that it already happened, and that's why there's been so much tension between the two of you. I didn't realize it was unresolved sexual tension," Dante says.

"Well, I hate to break it to you, but Nikki won."

Dante gives a weak shrug. He doesn't seem to care in the slightest. His pride isn't the least bit bruised.

"What'd you bet her?"

Do I even want to know what the stakes were in their little game?

"A massage, which always leads to sex with my little kitten," Dante says. "Seems like a win-win situation."

That was more information that I needed. "Right." I run a hand through my hair and glance at the door. A few more ladies enter the bar and join the girls, grabbing drinks.

They look just as young as the other ladies. They're all wearing fuck-me pumps or boots laced up to their knees. I shouldn't be turned on right now.

I hate myself.

I can't take it anymore. Being here makes me want to go home.

It takes everything in my power not to text her, call her, demand that she obey every instruction that I give her as her employer.

"I want Paige." The words come out as a growl. I'm a lion on the hunt, and the only meal that will satisfy me is *her*.

"I know."

He doesn't know.

Dante has no idea the attraction, desire, and pent-up frustration that tears at my insides.

I stand, ready to go and drop cash on the table for a tip. Dante gets the hint and escorts me outside to his car.

There's no knowing without a doubt that she wants me in return. I suspect that she does, that she's drawn to me the same as I am to her, but her desire to be around me could be strictly because of my daughter.

For all I know, tonight, when I slammed the door in her face, she wanted to talk about Nova.

She probably didn't want to talk about her attraction to me.

Well, fuck.

Fuck her.

She's going to talk.

I'll make her tell me everything.

Her desires. Her fantasies. The last time she touched herself. I want to know all of it, and I'll demand she tell me every dirty detail.

25

PAIGE

I'm awoken in the middle of the night by the click of a lock on the bedroom door.

I've always been a light sleeper, and being here is no different. Mostly, it's because I'm always listening for Nova.

The main door to my bedroom squeaks open, so I know it isn't Nova sneaking into my room.

"Moreno?"

I'm tired with sleep, and my eyes make out his outline as he approaches my bed.

It's him, but what is he doing coming in here in the middle of the night?

"You owe me the truth," Moreno says.

Isn't that what I've always done?

"I'd never lie to you." Well, except about Vance, but he doesn't know, he couldn't know.

"That's a lie," he says and laughs darkly. The closer he gets to my bed, I smell liquor on his breath.

I sit up, pulling the surrounding sheets. He'd never hurt me. I know that, but I'm not exactly comfortable with this position, either. I feel vulnerable and half-dressed while he's still fully clothed.

"You're drunk." It isn't intended as an accusation, but it does come out that way.

"It's hard not to be when the nanny steals my dead wife's wedding ring and wears it."

Guilt sweeps over me. I want to apologize, but how can I do that without letting him know that Nova was the one who took the ring?

She's been through so much, and I don't want to make things more difficult for her.

"You got the ring back," I say with as much conviction as I can muster. "Why does it bother you that I borrowed it?"

He laughs darkly and leans closer, sneering at me.

"Borrowed? You were wearing it! Are you trying to play house? Pretend to marry the mafia prince and live happily ever after."

"Mafia prince?" What the hell is he talking about? Has he lost his mind?

Wait.

Does that mean he works for the mafia?

I thought Nikki was ex-mafia, but that whatever empire they ran was legitimate and legal.

Shit.

What did I get myself involved in?

"Dante's the Don. Which makes him the king and Nikki, the queen. I'm the underboss, so I guess that makes me the prince." His brow furrows as he speaks like he realizes he may be saying too much.

I shift on the mattress, scooting back to get away from him.

Safety is my priority.

Being in this house, I no longer feel safe, especially with him.

"I want you, Paige." The heat from his words roars an inferno inside of me, but we can't. Before, he was just my boss, and that was way too complicated.

Knowing that he's also part of the mafia, I should get out while I still can.

While I'm still alive.

"You don't want me," I say. If his attention is on me, then he'll never let me go, and I'll never be free.

He stalks closer, leaning toward me, his hands on both sides of me, trapping me against the mattress.

His body is warm, and the heat radiates off him and onto me. "Tell me you don't want me, that you've never thought about me in a sexual way, and I'll never mention it again."

It should be so easy to lie, to tell him that he means nothing more to me than as a boss.

But the words don't come.

Not with his breath hovering and his lips within reach.

I want to kiss him, taste him, touch him, but he isn't the least bit sober, and I don't want him to regret anything between us.

"You're drunk," I say and gently push him away—my hand firm on his chest. "Go to sleep. In your bed." I hope he gets the message. It's not that I'm telling him no because I don't want him. I just don't want this being what we're about. I'm not some girl who he can call on when he's lonely or drunk.

He grumbles and pushes himself away from my bed.

I can't tell if it's the look of rejection crossing his features or something else. Anger? Resentment? Frustration?

Moreno is the hardest man to read. He gives no tells. He'd be great at a game of poker.

He stumbles out of my room without another word, shutting the door with an overzealous thud on the way out.

I don't know what to make of the situation. Will he even remember coming to me in the middle of the night?

26

MORENO

I royally fucked up.

My head throbs in a way that I can't even explain. I feel like I got run over by a bus, and someone scraped my ass off the ground and threw me on the floor of my bedroom.

Damn.

I didn't even make it into bed. But somehow, there's a pillow on the floor with me.

No wonder my head hurts. Every muscle aches inside of me as I stand and stretch. My stomach churns. I should grab water, crackers, and a few aspirin to ward off my drunken night.

I'm never going out with Dante again.

I strip down, shower, and even the hot water doesn't help relax me in the slightest.

It doesn't help that I went into Paige's bedroom last night.

Unless that was a dream?

It must have been a dream because she didn't slug me or tell me she hated me for the way that I've treated her.

Even the dream version of Paige is nice. Shit.

What did I do to deserve any ounce of kindness from her?

I dry off, dress, and head out into the hallway.

"Morning," Dante says and glances me over as he steps out of his bedroom. His white dress shirt is unbuttoned, and he's fixing his collar. He doesn't look quite ready for the day, but Nikki kicked him out of the bathroom if I had to guess.

Again.

I'm surprised with the renovations on the playroom and the panic room that he didn't install a bigger bathroom.

"You look like hell." Dante gives me a wicked grin. "What time did you roll into your bedroom last night?"

"What?" I rub the back of my neck, ruffled by his question. "After the bar with you, whatever time that was, boss."

Dante heads for the stairs, and I follow behind him. He's buttoning his dress shirt on the way downstairs.

"You and Paige had a late-night chat. I saw you sneak into her room when we got home. Well, sneak isn't exactly accurate. More like stumble into drunkenly and probably woke the neighbors."

And he didn't try to stop me?

"Thanks for looking out for me," I mutter under my breath.

We breeze through the foyer, and he slaps me on the back. "Anytime," Dante says.

"That was sarcasm. I shouldn't have gone into her bedroom drunk." Does he have any idea what a mess I made of the situation? I'm lucky if she still wants to work for me as Nova's nanny.

We head into the kitchen.

"I take it that your conversation didn't go well, professing your feelings for her?" Dante asks. He steps into the kitchen first and gives me an apologetic look.

Paige and Nova are at the high-top table having breakfast.

Paige's smile instantly disappears upon seeing me. She shifts in her seat to give Nova all her attention.

Shit.

It wasn't a dream. "Morning," I say to Paige and Nova as I brush past and make a bee-line for the coffee pot.

I grab a mug and hand one to Dante while he pours two cups of coffee, one for each of us.

"You should take the day off," Dante says. He's a little louder than I'd like, and I have the sneaking suspicion it's so that Paige will hear him.

Or I'm still hungover and everything feels amplified in intensity.

That possibility is just as likely.

I grab two aspirin from the cabinet and swallow them as the burning hot coffee forces me to wince in pain. A much-deserved suffering.

He shifts around, his back to the girls while he stares at me, keeping his voice much quieter. "Take the girls for a picnic lunch. Try to make a connection with Paige."

"You sound like I should join one of those dating shows on television. Does he have a connection with Paige, or will she break his heart?" I mock.

"I can hear you," Paige quips.

Shit.

My whispering voice is too loud.

I swallow my pride and stalk over to the table with Paige and Nova. "How does a picnic this afternoon with the three of us sound?"

My question is more for Nova, hoping to see her excitement about spending the day with me. I haven't spent as much time as I should with my daughter.

Nova looks so much like Serene that it's uncanny.

It makes moving on an impossible feat.

Nova glances at Paige. Is she seriously asking the nanny for permission?

What the hell have I done, bringing Paige into our home?

No doubt she's good with Nova, but the little girl is my child, and their connection—I can't help but feel a pang of jealousy at the relationship the two of them share.

Paige smiles warmly at Nova and hides any hint of annoyance with me. "That sounds like fun. Doesn't it?" she says, her attention on my daughter.

"Great." I sip my coffee and head for the entryway out of the kitchen.

"Maybe after, we can swing by the toy store," Paige says.

"Toy store?" I turn on my heel and spin around to face her.

That kind of suggestion should have been made with me privately, not in front of Nova. If I say no, I'll look like the bad guy. What game is Paige playing?

"Yeah, you know the place that has stuffed animals." Paige isn't paying attention to me. Her focus is entirely on Nova, and I see why.

My little one is practically bouncing in her seat. Like she wants to talk, but something is holding her back.

No kidding.

I'm the reason she's been silenced.

Children and the mafia don't mix. I don't know how Dante does it with Nikki and Luca. I envy his life, the fact that he can compartmentalize his job and family life so easily.

He fears nothing.

The job of a mob boss.

Protect his family at all costs.

I don't envy the job, the weight of the responsibility that falls entirely on his shoulders. Serene died because Vance wanted to even the score.

Vance is the scum-sucking vermin who sells women and children, traffics them through small towns, places where there aren't a lot of cops and visibility.

He runs a human trafficking ring, and while we put a serious dent in his operation in Breckenridge, slaughtering his men and the don's home, they're still out there.

For years, they've left town, probably attempting to keep a low profile. But seeing Vance at the club Dante owns, without a doubt, he's back.

Vance doesn't show up without a plan. I just don't know what that plan is, and that's why I don't like the idea of letting Nova go to the toy store.

It's the kind of place that draws too much attention to the situation. Anyplace public puts Paige and Nova at risk.

Keeping them locked up in the cabin at the compound is for the best. It's keeping them both safe, but I know Paige doesn't understand, let alone see it that way. She thinks I'm punishing her by not letting her leave.

Dante's idea for a picnic lunch is dangerous if we engage in it outside of our grounds. I planned on having it outside, safely inside the gates where guards can assure Paige and Nova's safety.

"What do you say?" Paige asks again, a friendly smile on her face. "We can have a picnic at the park and visit the toy store across the street. It's a short walk."

Everything inside of me screams that this is a bad idea. But Nova's eyes are bright and cheerful.

It's been too long since I've seen a smile graze her features. I can't say no to Nova.

We can bring extra guards and security to watch over us.

I take a long swig of my coffee. "It's a date."

27

PAIGE

I didn't think Moreno would agree to a picnic, let alone taking Nova to the toy store afterward.

With Dante, his boss in the room, maybe he couldn't say no? Especially to the picnic idea, which was not Moreno's plan.

I won't hold that against him. At least he agreed to an afternoon outside the cabin and away from the men in suits.

The mafia.

I shiver, just thinking about last night and his confession.

Moreno is a mafia prince.

Was he serious or so far drunk that even he was rattling off nonsense?

Either seemed completely plausible, and while I want answers, I also won't ask those types of questions in front of Nova. She's young and impressionable, and I don't need to make her fear her father.

From the moment I first met her, it already seemed like that was the case. But lately, she's softened around him and vice versa.

At least from the small and short, intimate moments that I've seen.

Moreno has been avoiding me for the past week. Until last night, when he snuck into my bedroom unannounced and proclaimed his feelings for me.

The tension between us is undeniable. He remembers what happened last night.

I wasn't sure if he would.

He relents about the toy store and picnic before disappearing out of the kitchen. I've never seen him run so fast to get away from me.

Well, he can't avoid me forever.

––––––––––

"I thought we were going on a picnic, just the three of us?" I emphasize as I glance in the side mirror.

There's a black SUV following us with three guards in suits.

They do not look the least bit discreet. If Moreno wants to bring attention to himself, he sure knows how.

"We are, but I have to know that we're going to be safe when we're in town." He pulls out past the main gates that are already open for us to leave.

I glance at him. "Why wouldn't we be safe?" I'm waiting for him to tell me what he does for a living, that he's an underboss for the mafia.

But the air is thick, and I'm met with silence.

"I just want to protect my family," Moreno says.

I get that. I understand his concern and fear. It's relatable, especially after the club and then the fire. However, the second was entirely caused by accident. But it still didn't make it any less frightening.

"Because you're the mafia," I whisper, making sure Moreno hears me, but with the radio on, I doubt Nova can hear a word from the backseat.

She's buckled into her car seat, oblivious to the conversation commencing between us.

I glance back at her and offer a warm smile.

Nova stares out the window, watching the scenery.

Oblivious.

Good.

"Where did you hear that?" Moreno asks, his tone sharp.

He doesn't deny it.

His jaw is firm and tight. He grips the steering wheel hard as we head along the gravel road for the main thoroughfare.

"From you." I purse my lips together, considering whether I should remind him of his words, *mafia prince*.

His eyes flinch. "You're mistaken."

Denial.

Okay, two can play at that game. "You're right. I must be mistaken." I shift in the passenger seat and turn slightly to stare at him.

I don't let him get away that easily with his lies.

"Just like you didn't come into my room last night and profess your feelings toward me. That you want me, and you're a mafia prince."

He swallows, and I swear there's a trickle of sweat glistening on his forehead.

"Is it hot in here?" He reaches for the thermostat on the vehicle and cranks the air.

I'm not wrong.

He shoots me a look as he turns up the air conditioning. "Don't ever repeat what you said unless you want to get yourself killed."

I push the vents away from me. "Is that a threat?"

Would Moreno hurt me?

Kill me?

I've been around him long enough that I don't fear him. Maybe I should. I haven't seen that wicked side of him, but if he is a mafia prince, then he's bound to have blood on his hands.

"I'm trying to protect you," Moreno says with a warning. "If you're not careful, you'll end up trusting the wrong men, and they will hurt you. That's why I have guards accompanying us off the grounds."

Moreno clears his throat and is quick to change the subject. "We have another appointment with the therapist this Friday."

Great.

"And you're expecting me to accompany you again as your wife?" I rub the back of my neck. I'm not the least bit okay with lying about being Nova's mother.

How can we help Nova if we're lying to the therapist?

"I don't see another choice," Moreno says. "Unless you want me to tell her that you're sick this week or have a migraine. But you're going to have to come to the next appointment after that."

A laugh slips out past my lips at the absurdity of his suggestion. "Or you could try telling her the truth. Not your strong suit, though."

He flinches at my remark.

It looks like I hit a nerve.

Good. Maybe he'll consider taking my comments seriously. I don't want to see Nova strung along when she could be getting whatever help she needs.

And it's clear to me, having heard her humming a song and Ariella's remark that Nova used to speak, I can only surmise that something tragic happened.

"It's her mother, isn't it?"

"What?" Moreno glances at me as we pull up at the park.

"The reason that she doesn't speak anymore. Her mother died and she misses her."

He shuts off the engine of the car. "Yes." He's a little too quick to answer. Moreno climbs out of the car and opens the back door, unbuckling Nova as he helps her out of her car seat. He grabs a blanket, and she runs off toward the jungle gym.

"Be careful!" Moreno shouts at Nova.

She waves him off dismissively.

I try not to laugh. The smirk is impossible to remove from my face while I grab the picnic lunch in the backseat and follow Moreno onto the grass under a tree for shade.

We're well within eyeshot of Nova with a good view of her playing, and we also have three guards spreading out, making sure we're safe, along with Nova.

It was weird to have Leone accompany Nova and me to the park when I met Ariella, but this feels even more obtrusive.

Although we don't have privacy visually, none of the guards are hovering or lingering over us. We can talk amongst each other without anyone eavesdropping.

Moreno lays out the blanket while I unpack our lunch and have a seat. With Nova playing and giving us a little time alone, it's now or never if I'm going to question him about his mafia dealings.

"So, you're a mafia prince."

He glances up at me, unamused. "You're not going to let it go."

"Well, no. Honestly, I don't think I can."

It's a big ball that he dropped last night, along with wanting me. However, I'm not sure if that was the alcohol talking or him.

Does he still want to be with me?

"It doesn't come with a crown," Moreno says. He points to the top of his head.

"Is that a joke?" I ask. I'm not laughing. I take a bite of one of the sandwiches that we brought. Right now, I'd gladly do anything to cut the tension brewing between us.

I know that it's not just me. He feels it too, and acknowledging that feels almost like too much.

"Mafia gets such a bad rap. We're not bad guys. Well, most of us," Moreno says.

I don't believe him. I feel like he's trying to convince me to trust him because I live with him, work for him, and there's no way out.

I don't know why I ask it, but the words come out quicker than I intend. "So, you've never killed anyone?"

28

MORENO

What is it with Paige and her twenty questions?

I need to take control of the conversation and steer it far from what happened last night. Not talking about it is the best option.

I should never have gone into her bedroom.

Confessing to being a mafia prince. What the fuck was I thinking?

Oh, right? I wasn't thinking.

I was drunk and hoping Paige would admit that she wanted me as bad as I wanted her.

What are we, in high school again?

I take what I want.

But I won't force myself on her.

"Well, have you ever killed anyone?" Paige asks me again when I haven't answered her quickly enough. "Or is silence your admission of guilt?" She tilts her head just slightly.

I reach out and brush a strand of hair behind her ear, tucking it back.

A part of me expects her to pull away or flinch.

Paige doesn't.

Instead, she leans in and exhales a soft sigh. "I am truly sorry about the ring."

I withdraw my hand and land it back in my lap. If I focus on eating, then at least I won't say anything I regret. I open a bottle of water and shove it against my lips.

Maybe my silence will encourage her to elaborate, to speak, to explain why the hell she felt it necessary to snoop through my drawers and steal my dead wife's ring.

If I'm not careful, I'll finish the entire bottle of water before I take a bite of my sandwich.

"I wish I could explain it all to you so that you'd realize I'm not a thief. I'm just trying to do the right thing," she says.

My eyes narrow and twitch. I close the lid on the water bottle.

"Are you going to say anything?" Paige asks.

At least the conversation isn't about me being a mafia prince anymore.

I focus on my lunch, having a bite, smiling through closed lips, and I point at my mouth.

"Convenient," she mutters under her breath.

I open the bottle of water and take a swig while she eats small bites of her sandwich. It's nothing fancy, but I also wasn't planning on having a picnic lunch before the idea was thrown at me like a water balloon. There was no getting out of the way of the impending splash.

"I don't know how you're trying to do the right thing unless you spell it out for me," I say. Maybe if I clarify that I have no idea why she'd steal from me, she'll elaborate. "Is it because of Ariella?"

It's a stab in the dark.

Her brow furrows. "Why would you think that?" Paige takes a swig of her water before screwing the lid back on the bottle.

"Seems like she'd ask for dirt on me," I say with a shrug.

I'm trying to fathom a reasonable excuse for what she did, except I can't find one. No one else in the Ricci home would steal from me. No one is stupid enough to betray me.

Except for Nova.

Aww, fuck me.

"It has nothing to do with Ariella," Paige says. Her voice is soft and calm, and her gaze is locked on mine.

My stomach does somersaults. I can't take another bite, and I put the remainder of my uneaten meal back into the plastic baggie.

"You're covering for Nova."

I'm an idiot for not seeing it sooner.

I didn't want to see it.

Paige's gaze falls to her lap, and she undoes the lid on her water and brings it back to her lips.

Silence.

"Please, tell me you're not covering for my daughter." Honestly, I don't know which is worse: Nova stole her mother's ring or that Paige lied to me to protect my daughter.

"You wanted someone to blame," Paige says and glances at the jungle gym.

Nova is climbing the rope ladder, clutching it as she makes it to the top.

My girl seems to have no fear. Impossible, considering all that she's been through. It's like she's channeling her silence and mutism into something else.

Bravery?

In a matter of weeks, since meeting Paige, I don't even recognize Nova.

Physically, of course, she's the same little girl who is my daughter. But she's trying new things, coming out of her shell, no longer hiding and avoiding me.

Paige is good for Nova.

"I'm sorry I doubted you and accused you of stealing from me." An apology is the least that I owe her. I'm lucky she hasn't already quit.

Paige offers me a warm smile. "Well, I *was* wearing the ring."

"Yes." I nod slowly. "And why were you wearing it?"

"I spoke with Nova and asked her to turn the ring over to me. Once I had it in my possession, I didn't want to lose it. I planned on returning it to you the next morning when I saw you."

Her story sounds plausible. "You didn't plan on me coming into your bedroom."

"Precisely. I never meant to hurt you, and I know that Nova has been through so much already. I didn't want your anger directed at her. We talked and she won't be stealing anything again."

"She talked to you?"

"Well, no." Paige purses her lips. "I spoke with her, but she understood what she did was wrong. Now that I've answered your questions, I want you to answer mine. How long have you been a mafia prince?"

I shake my head and wag my finger at her. "That's not how this works."

I'm not answering her questions.

"Why not?" She pouts.

I'm not sure whether she's emphasizing her discontent, or it comes naturally, but it's freaking adorable.

My body reacts, my cock stirring in my trousers.

"Nova!" I wave at my daughter and gesture for her to come join us.

Paige scrunches her nose like a little kid, and I try not to laugh. Nova is rubbing off on Paige as much as Paige is on Nova. It's endearing, mostly.

Nova flies down the slide and stumbles, tripping over her feet. She waits for a second, realizing she isn't hurt, and then stands and finishes her sprint over to us.

"Come have lunch," I say.

Paige stares at me.

She probably knows what I'm doing—avoiding the conversation that she wants to have. Like I told her, that's not how this works. I'm not going to answer her questions about the mafia. Certainly not out in public, and not while she could be wearing a wire.

I trust Paige, but that doesn't mean someone else might not have gotten to her before we met.

It's a leap for sure, but not everyone can be trusted, and she was brought into the family and hired as my daughter's nanny. She doesn't need to know anything about the business or my position in it.

Nova plops herself down between us, and I unwrap a peanut butter and jelly sandwich for her from a plastic baggie.

She sits crisscross and quietly munches on her lunch. Not that I expect her to speak. I've grown accustomed to her silence. That's not to say that I don't want her to speak. I'm not a monster. But if she did start talking about what happened, I'm not sure how to deal with it, the trauma, any of what she may have witnessed.

"Is that good?" I smile weakly at Nova.

She glances up with wide eyes and takes another bite. She's got strawberry jelly on her fingers and a smidgeon on her cheek.

Thankfully, I remembered an extra pack of wipes and many napkins to help clean her up before leaving.

Bang!

Bang!

Bang!

Nova bursts into tears and jumps into Paige's lap.

Shit.

29

PAIGE

Several firecrackers are shot off, and one of the guards rushes over, gun drawn at a bunch of teenagers behind a tree.

"What the hell are you doing?" Moreno jumps up to deescalate the situation before it gets even more out of hand.

Bruno, the guard, puts the safety back on and shoves the gun under his jacket, hidden from view.

Does he carry that everywhere with him? Maybe I should have expected it. He is a guard, but shouldn't he still recognize the difference between a firecracker and a gunshot?

Nova is curled in my arms, sobbing.

Gently, I rub her back as she clings to me with sticky fingers from her peanut butter and jelly sandwich. I seem to be wearing the jelly as much as Nova.

Moreno reams out the guard before approaching us. He squats and I hear his knees crack. "Hey, Nova." His voice is soft and soothing as he tries to get her attention.

She's buried her face in my neck and doesn't so much as glance up at her father.

"Maybe give her a few minutes," I offer as a suggestion. She's worked up and needs a little time to calm down.

He's fuming under his breath and stands, stalking over toward the guard who lost his cool.

Nova peeks for a second to witness her father's wrath, directed at the guard.

"Hey. Do you want to go to the toy store?" I ask, hoping to draw her attention back to me.

She emits a loud sigh and glances up with wide eyes. Nova gives a faint nod before cuddling me again, her arms tight around my chest.

———

"I'm sorry about that back there," Moreno says as he opens the glass door. The bell on the door jingles.

I carry Nova into the store, her arms tight around my neck.

"It's safe in here," I assure her. "How about I put you down and let you walk around and pick out a toy?"

I probably should have spoken to Moreno about my offer for her to buy a present before stepping into the shop, but what did he expect? You can't bring a kid into a toy store and leave empty-handed.

Certainly not a four-year-old.

Besides, after the picnic we just endured, I don't think he'll say no.

"Keep an eye on her," Moreno says as I step into the small shop.

I wasn't planning on abandoning Nova.

He heads outside, and by the looks of it, he's giving hell to the guard who pulled his gun.

Good.

Nova slips her hand in mine, and I walk her farther inside the store so that she doesn't see her father screaming at the guard. She's been through enough today.

One trauma at a time.

She tugs on my hand and pulls me to follow her down the stuffed animal aisle.

She has an entire collection of stuffed toys back at home. The kid could seriously run a zoo, but she doesn't have any trouble finding a baby gorilla on the shelf. She points at it as it's out of her reach, and I quickly glance at the price tag before handing it to her.

Even if Moreno doesn't agree to pay for it, I'll buy Nova the present with my stipend. I have a few dollars, and the kid is deserving.

"Can I?" Nova asks, her voice soft. I barely hear her, but the fact she's asking me a question and speaking has my heart pitter-pattering in my chest.

I don't want to make a big deal out of it. The last thing I want is for her to clam up and become silent because of my stupidity.

"Of course," I say, as if her speaking for the first time since we've been together isn't a life-changing event.

For her, maybe it isn't. If Ariella was right and Nova used to speak, she's probably dying to unload whatever is going on, and I'll be there for her every step of the way.

She squeezes my hand and clutches the baby gorilla to her chest. The kid isn't parting with it, and the shop owner is super sweet and understanding, offering to cut off the tags carefully while letting Nova hold the toy in her arms.

"Thank you," I say.

"Anything for Mr. Ricci," the woman says.

"You know Moreno?"

"Yes, of course. His family has been through so much. It's good to see he's moving on. You make a beautiful family."

I open my mouth to correct her but think better of it. "Thank you," I say. While I don't want to start any rumors, I also don't need to explain to this stranger that I'm Nova's nanny, either.

Nova opts to hold her new friend tight in her arms instead of putting it in a bag.

Hopefully, Moreno is done shouting at the young guard. The last thing I want is to scare Nova again. She's finally all smiles, and the fear from earlier seems to have been forgotten.

Nova clings to her new toy while we step outside into the sun.

The blanket and picnic have already been cleaned up, and Moreno is waiting outside alone.

Where are the guards?

I glance around briefly but don't see any of them. Maybe he told them to leave and head back to the cabin?

Moreno bends down to Nova's level as we approach. "I see you made a new friend." He offers her a reassuring smile, but she doesn't speak.

I almost feel like I imagined her voice, her soft words that spilled past her lips.

But I know it wasn't a daydream.

I'll have to tell Moreno, but not now. Not in front of Nova. I don't want to make her uncomfortable or have her feel that she can't trust me.

Am I betraying her by confiding in Moreno?

———————

I'm exhausted, and Nova can barely keep her eyes open as I read her a bedtime story. Her gorilla is tucked under her arm. Beside her, are six other plush friends joining her in bed tonight.

Every night, it's a new toy plus her favorite giraffe, which is still beside her, tucked under the covers.

Her eyes keep fluttering closed, and as soon as I turn the page, she wakes herself back up.

The kid doesn't want to sleep. She's fighting it with every ounce of strength within her.

Her father hasn't come in to tuck her into bed yet. He usually comes by late, after she's asleep and he's done working.

But Dante gave him the day off.

I half expect that he'll come in during her bedtime ritual and join us, but he hasn't yet.

What's keeping him?

Nova sighs softly and pats my arm.

I glance from the book to the little girl with a pouting bottom lip jutting out.

"I don't want to sleep," Nova whispers.

Again, I try not to hide my surprise or my overzealous joy that she's speaking with me. "What's wrong?" I ask. My voice is soft and gentle, calm.

I close the book but leave my hand in to save the page if she wants me to keep reading. Although, I could have sworn she'd have fallen asleep before we reached the end of the book.

"Bad dreams," Nova whispers.

"Do you have a lot of bad dreams?" I ask. Not once, has she snuck into my bedroom during the night. I've assumed that she's been sound asleep and all right.

Maybe she just didn't feel safe and comfortable.

Nova shrugs, avoiding an answer.

"I have an idea," I say and stand.

She sits up, a frown on her face. Nova looks terrified that I'm leaving her after she just confessed something so deep and intimate.

I hurry into my bedroom and am quick in the bathroom. I reach under the sink for a spray that I picked up. It smells of citrus and sage.

I'm back beside her bed within a minute, and I crank the window open a few inches.

I spray around the open window frame. The smell isn't overly strong and is quite pleasant.

She breathes deeply, taking in the scent.

"Do you believe in magic?" I ask.

If she doesn't, she will tonight.

"Magic?" Nova's eyes widen, and her face lights up as she tightens her hold on her gorilla.

"Yes," I whisper, keeping my voice down. Someone is bound to notice the two of us chatting, especially if one of the guards is stationed outside the bedroom.

I spray a few more times around the room, near her bed.

"Bad dreams go away," I say. "We only want good dreams and happy thoughts in this house. Anything bad or gloomy leave right now."

Nova scrunches her face and smiles. She points to the window. "Leave, bad dreams!" she says with a squeal.

I smile and mist a few more times near the bathroom and then the main door of the bedroom.

The young girl settles back down under the covers, and I close the window once we are both satisfied the bad dreams have left the room.

"Goodnight." I tuck Nova into bed and plant a soft kiss on her cheek. "Sweet dreams, and if you need anything, I'm just next door. You can come find me. Okay?"

"Okay." Nova rolls onto her stomach to get comfy.

I close the bedroom door between us, quiet so not to disturb her, even though she hasn't fallen asleep yet.

"Hey," Moreno's voice startles me.

"How long have you been in here?" I ask, the spray in my hand.

"Does that really ward off bad dreams?"

Did he hear that? Then he heard Nova speak.

Why hasn't he said anything about that yet?

Maybe he didn't hear Nova. She's soft-spoken and quiet. It's possible he only heard me through the door.

"Well, it doesn't hurt," I say. "Do you want to tuck her into bed? She just closed her eyes."

Moreno gives a faint nod and brushes past me, his touch warming something inside, stirring a fire within me.

Why does he make me feel this way?

Conflicted.

Desiring him is a disaster waiting to happen. I should let him go. Only be a nanny for his little girl. It would be safer, less dangerous.

He quietly opens the adjoining door and sneaks in to give a goodnight kiss to Nova.

I try not to eavesdrop on their special moment together, but I find it difficult to tear my gaze away from the open door and Moreno tucking his daughter into bed.

He's warmed up so much toward Nova since the first day I met him. I'm not sure what's changed. Has he realized what he's been missing out on? Maybe his wife had always been the warm and compassionate one with Nova.

Moreno tucks her in and retreats from the bedroom, quietly closing the door as he's invited himself once again into my personal space.

For the first time, I don't mind it. But my stomach is fluttering with nervousness.

How do I tell him Nova spoke to me today?

Will he be angry that it was me instead of him?

30

MORENO

There's a firm knock on the office door. "Sir, you need to come here at once," Rhys interrupts.

Dante and I both glance up at Rhys and exchange a worried look.

Has Vance finally come for retribution?

He murdered my wife, Serene, and our previous nanny, Laura. Vengeance should be mine, but he won't stop until he's destroyed our family and burned our home to the ground.

Dante stands.

"I need Moreno," Rhys says.

"What's going on?" Worry bolts through me like lightning. I stand in haste, nearly toppling the chair over.

"I was standing guard outside Nova's bedroom, and I swear I heard her and the nanny talking."

I press my lips together and breeze right out of Dante's office.

I'm done with work. He gave me the day off, and the two of us were playing catch up, but that can wait.

If Nova is finally opening up and back to her old self, I want to see it for myself.

I'm hurrying up the stairs, and I hear Dante's voice behind me.

"Tread carefully, Moreno."

I didn't even realize he was following me until he spoke. I glance over my shoulder at him as I hurry down the hallway. "What are you suggesting?"

"Just wait outside," he says and holds up a hand. "If you charge in there, you could crumble everything good that's happening right now."

He's right.

I know Dante wants what's best for Nova, but I'm her father.

She should be speaking to me!

My heart hurts just thinking that she trusts the nanny more than her flesh and blood. What have I done?

I run a hand through my hair and groan. I'm trying not to stomp or yank the door open as I approach Nova's bedroom.

Muffled sounds are coming from inside the room. It's difficult to make out what's being said, but there is a conversation happening, and it's not just Paige reading Nova a bedtime story.

I've listened to a few of her stories from just outside the door, and while she may attempt to do different voices for the characters, none sound like Nova.

I opt to slip into Paige's bedroom. If she's talking to Nova, then I can hear what's being said.

Am I eavesdropping?

Yes, but it's worth the risk of getting caught.

Paige will have to get over it.

I close the door, not letting Dante have any further involvement. His opinion, he can keep to himself.

I want to burst through the adjoining door. My heart hammers in my chest at Nova's sweet squeal.

The air is sucked from my lungs.

My feet are frozen in place.

I can't move.

I can't breathe.

A moment later, and Paige steps into the bedroom. She seems mildly surprised to see me.

There's so much that I want to say, but not yet. I need to see Nova, tuck her into bed, and I hope that in a halfway state of slumber, she'll return the words that I voice.

I brush past Paige and into Nova's room. I fix her covers, although they're already neat, and drop a kiss on her forehead. "Goodnight, Nova. I love you."

Without a sound, I ease back away from the bed and with soft steps retreat into Paige's room.

I could exit through the bedroom door, but I don't want to do that, not yet.

Paige and I have a lot to discuss. I shut the door behind myself as I join her in her bedroom. Usually, she's in her pajamas under the covers, reading a book.

Tonight, I've surprised her.

At least I hope that I have and she's happy to see me.

"Do you want to sit?" she asks and gestures to her bed.

"How long has Nova been speaking to you?" I don't intend for it to come out as an accusation, but saying I'm not jealous is a lie.

She exhales a heavy sigh and plops onto the edge of the mattress.

There's too much energy pulsating through my body. I'm incapable of sitting still, and so I tower above her. It takes everything in me not to pace the length of her bedroom.

I need to remain calm and quiet.

Nova is asleep right next door, and the walls are thin enough that I could wake her. That's the last thing I want to happen.

Paige fiddles with her hands on her lap. "Just today. She asked if she could have the stuffed animal at the toy store."

"Thank you for buying that for her. Let me know what it costs, and I'll reimburse you." It didn't even occur that I'd left it up to the nanny to pay for my child's toy. I shouldn't have done that. It was irresponsible.

"It's not a big deal." She waves her hand dismissively into the air.

"Nova talking again is a big deal."

"Again?" Paige tilts her head, staring up at me with wide eyes. "Oh, I agree. Nova talking is a big deal. What's this again thing?"

Fuck.

Caught in a lie.

Not that I should have ever lied to Paige, but I didn't expect Nova would open up again. After a year of mutism, I thought that was it, and she was just going to be silent.

What did I know about kids? Serene had always been a loving and doting parent. She wanted kids. I didn't know how the hell to change a diaper, let alone deal with a four-year-old who refused to speak.

Honestly, I thought she'd grow out of it after a week. That it was because her mother died. Boy, was I wrong.

"After Serene—her mother—died, she refused to speak."

"And you didn't think to take her to a therapist after her mother's death?" Paige asks.

My mouth is dry. I rub my hands together, wrestling inwardly with my demons. "It wasn't that simple. Neither of us wanted to talk about it."

"*You* didn't want to talk about it. That girl needed her father," Paige says.

I give her credit for standing up to me and saying what no one else had the courage to a year ago, to my face.

"She still needs her father," I say. "And I'm here."

Paige folds her arms across her chest and emits a heavy sigh. Her lips are pressed together.

Does she not believe me?

"I'm trying. Having my wife murdered and the nanny slaughtered, possibly in front of Nova, isn't exactly in the 'how to be a dad' handbook," I mock.

She stands. Her brow is furrowed. Paige steps closer, coming face-to-face with me. "You forgot to mention your previous nanny was murdered."

I cringe.

Shit.

There I go, slipping up again.

"It wasn't a hot selling point for the job," I say.

Paige must realize that I couldn't put that in the job listing or talk about it. I hadn't intended for her to discover her employer was the mafia. That wasn't a conversation to be had during a job interview.

"I get that, but you have a duty to be honest with me." She doesn't back down.

I shake my head and take a tentative step back. I need to turn this whole thing around and gain control again. I don't like that she has my wheels spinning and my heart racing.

"No."

"No?" she asks. "You're not going to be honest with me? Then, I quit!"

Her boldness has me taken aback for a brief second.

"You can't quit. You signed a contract, Paige, and in case you forgot, you aren't to be released from your contract without it being either in agreement, my decision, or until a replacement is hired."

"Fine, then hire a replacement!" She throws her arms up into the air, exasperated.

That's not going to happen.

I don't want anyone else with my daughter.

"No. Nova is finally opening up, talking, and you want to abandon her?" I turn the tables on Paige.

Her shoulders slump. Defeated. "That's not fair."

"No, it's not fair to Nova. She looks up to you. Dare I say the kid loves you."

Paige licks her lips and takes a step away from me. "I won't work for a liar," Paige says.

"I've only kept things from you to protect you." That's all I've ever wanted, her well-being.

Well, Nova and hers.

"You can't quit, Paige. I don't accept your resignation."

She exhales a heavy sigh and heads back toward the mattress, slumping down on the bed. "Fine, but I want this weekend off, and I want to be allowed to leave the cabin and the premises. No guards."

She's not a prisoner, but letting her leave alone puts her at risk.

"I can't do that."

31

PAIGE

"You can't let me leave?" I scoff. "Or you won't? How am I not being held captive if I can't leave?"

"Didn't you hear what I said happened to the last nanny? She was murdered." Moreno steps closer. "My job is to protect you. Your job is to look after my daughter. Let me do my job and I won't interfere in yours."

I laugh under my breath.

"Seriously?"

I don't believe him.

The nerve of him to not let me leave the premises!

"You can't keep me here, Moreno."

"I'm trying to protect you. Remember Vance, at the club? The fact that you work for me, the Ricci family, makes you a target."

I purse my lips together. "What if I'm willing to take the risk?" Vance wouldn't hurt me. If he wanted to kill me, he'd have done it when I walked into his agency and requested an application to become a nanny.

Right?

Except I didn't mean a damned thing to the Ricci family before I became their nanny. Is that why I'm a target now?

Moreno has to be overreacting. Not that I blame him because I don't. He has been through a lot, with his wife having died and the previous nanny being murdered.

His tongue darts out along the side of his mouth for a second as he's thinking about my proposition.

Will he let me leave?

"No."

"Come on." I'm trying not to whine, but he's infuriating to be around. "You can't keep me hostage."

"You're not a hostage. You're an employee of the Ricci family. As far as I see it, you have a roof over your head, a warm bed, the entire house as your castle, and great company." He smirks at me, and all I want to do is wipe that grin right from his face.

"Fine."

If he doesn't let me leave, then I'll sneak out.

Or convince one of the guards that Moreno is letting me leave.

He cocks an eyebrow at me. "Good. I'm glad that's settled." He seems mildly surprised that I give in to him.

"You can have the weekend off, but you're not leaving the cabin unless I come with you or one of the guards accompanies you."

There's not a chance that he'd be on board with me hanging out with Ariella. It's best if I keep the arrangement to myself.

"Fine."

————

I text Ariella and make lunch plans for just the two of us at a small café in town. She gives me the address.

Glancing at my watch, if I leave now, I can make it a few minutes early.

There isn't traffic to worry about, just interference from the guards.

Nova is having a day out with Moreno. He took at least one guard with him, possibly two.

I head for the front door, keys in hand, my purse slung over my shoulder.

Rhys catches sight of me as I grab the front door handle. "Where are you going?" he asks.

There's a frown etched on his face. He seems unsure of protocol, which I use to my advantage.

"Moreno wanted me to run to the store to pick up some new supplies for Nova. Finger paints, a canvas, you know, the usual art stuff that kids love."

I turn the handle and open the door. "I'll be back after lunch."

"Is someone supposed to accompany you?" Rhys asks. "Don Ricci always insists that a guard accompanies his wife off the premises."

I smile reassuringly. "You don't have to worry. I'm not Nikki, the don's wife. I'm just the nanny." With as much conviction, I try to let him know that he doesn't need to babysit me.

There's still confliction etched on his face. "Okay." He answers a little too quickly. He seems to still be mulling it over in his head, his brow furrowed. "Maybe I should call—"

I'm out the door and slam it shut before he can finish his sentence.

If he does call Moreno, I don't want to be around. I'll handle his wrath later when he sees that I'm fine, and he was overreacting.

Hurrying to my car, I unlock the driver's side door and hop in, starting the engine. I put the car in gear and back out, heading down the main path for the guard gate.

The guard opens the gate and gives me a nod without so much as a second thought.

That was easy!

I laugh under my breath, hit the gas, and head away from the cabin.

I glance in the rearview, expecting someone to chase after me, tell me that I can't leave without a guard or Moreno's approval.

Dust and dirt kick up behind me.

No one appears to be following.

———

I pull into the parking lot, then head into the café and spot Ariella at a table. Her husband has the kids today, which is a nice break for both of us.

"I'm glad you managed to show up," Ariella says with a warm smile. She stands and gives me a huge embrace. "I thought that you'd text to cancel on me."

I'm not sure I want to tell her that I was worried that might happen too. "Well, I made it," I say with a laugh.

I scoot into the booth, sitting across from her.

"How's working for you know who?" she says and grins.

At least she knows how to be somewhat discreet and not announce the family's name I'm employed under.

"He's a handful." I laugh. "More than the kid."

Ariella chuckles. "Well, anytime you need a break, you are invited to crash at our place. We have a guest bedroom that you can occupy."

"Appreciated."

The waitress approaches our table, brings us menus, and rattles off the specials. After letting her know that I need a few minutes to decide, she rushes off to help another couple at a table.

"How is Nova doing?" Ariella asks, keeping her voice down.

I appreciate her discretion.

"She started talking again. Just this past week."

Ariella's eyes are wide, and she's staring at me in apparent disbelief. "Wow. That's great. She's such a sweetheart. I'll bet her father is happy too."

I press my lips tight together for a brief moment, and Ariella seems to catch my silence as concern.

"Oh no. Does he not know that she's talking? Or is he worried about what she'll say?"

I shake my head. "No, he's ecstatic, but she hasn't spoken to him yet. Most of our conversations are just between the two of us or her and one of her stuffed animals."

"That girl loves her giraffe," Ariella says. "I remember she used to carry that to the playground. It would irritate Serene and Laura. They'd always worry that she'd leave it behind."

"Laura?"

"Her last nanny."

Moreno hasn't been forthcoming with information about his wife's death or the nanny's murder. I've tried to give him time, but I want more details. A part of me needs to know what I might be up against.

"Were you friends with Serene and Laura?" I ask.

The waitress decides now is an excellent time to reappear, and I scan the menu to find something suitable. I order an avocado salad and a glass of water before handing my menu back to the waitress.

"Serene and I never really conversed. Laura and I would chit-chat when the kids played in the park. Laura was a sweet girl, young, and looked a lot like

Nikki, now that I think about it. The same hair and build. She could have easily been mistaken from behind."

"You think that's why she was—" I try to keep my voice barely above a whisper. I don't finish with the word that I want to: *murdered*.

I'm concerned someone might overhear.

She leans forward and plants her hands on the table. "I do. Did he tell you about that night?"

The waitress brings over two glasses of water to the table, along with silverware. We both smile politely, making sure not to discuss Moreno, Serene, or Nova in front of her. She probably wouldn't say anything, but you can't be too certain.

The moment she walks away, I exhale a breath. "No, he hasn't said anything about that night." I haven't exactly asked him, either, about the murder. While I had known his wife died, it wasn't until recently that I'd been made aware there had been a previous nanny who had been murdered.

My stomach is in knots just thinking about what might have happened.

Maybe I should have taken Moreno's advice and brought one of the guards to the café. He didn't have to sit with us. He could have grabbed his own table, had lunch, and just kept an eye on anyone suspicious.

I am paranoid.

Glancing around the café, there doesn't appear to be anyone interested in the two of us or our conversation.

Ariella tugs her bottom lip between her teeth. "You should probably ask him. I mean, I've heard things from Jaxson and the guys at Eagle Tactical."

"Jaxson?" I repeat the name over on my tongue. I went to school with a kid by that name, and I wouldn't have thought twice about it, except I'd run into a gentleman by the same first name.

It had to be him. "Wait. Are you married to Jaxson Monroe?"

"Yes, why?" Ariella asks with a nervous smile.

"Tall, muscular, has lots of tattoos?" I can't fathom that there are two Jaxson Monroes in Breckenridge. Hell, there's probably not even two Jaxsons in all of town. There certainly weren't when I was a kid.

She laughs under her breath.

The waitress brings our meals to the table, and the conversation silences once again until we're left alone.

Ariella leans forward. "You know my husband. How? Please, tell me he's not working with Dante." The color drains right from her face.

"Gosh, no!" I gesture wildly with my hands before reaching for my fork. "That is not what I meant. I grew up in Breckenridge. On my first day back in town, I ran into Jaxson at a coffee shop. He recognized me."

Ariella exhales a soft sigh and her shoulders slump, looking a bit more relaxed. "Oh, that's nice." She takes a sip of her water as the color comes back into her cheeks even more.

"I felt bad," I further explain. "I didn't recognize him. Certainly not with the tattoos."

"And I'll bet he didn't have a six-pack in high school, either," Ariella says with a grin.

I shake my head. "Definitely not." Most of the guys in school, I wasn't attracted to. I'd been chasing college boys outside of town. Big mistake. They were all heartbreakers.

"You should come over for dinner."

I glance at my watch as I finish the last few bites of salad. "I appreciate the offer, but I can't. I usually watch the little one around the clock. I'm lucky to have today and tomorrow off."

"Bring her with you. Just maybe leave her dad at home," Ariella says and scrunches her nose.

I try not to take offense at her suggestion. It's not like she knows anything is happening between Moreno and me. Hell, I'm not even sure I know what's going on between us.

It's complicated.

Two words that are like the heaviest of rain clouds ready to pour down atop us. "You know, he's not that bad of a guy," I say, finding myself defending Moreno.

I shouldn't defend him.

He wouldn't even let me leave on my own.

Reaching for my water glass, I down the last remnants. Just thinking about him, my mouth is dry, my throat parched.

"He's your boss," Ariella reminds me with not even a tiny bit of subtlety.

Crap.

Moreno isn't even in the room with us and she's reminding me that I'm his employee. It must be unmistakable, my feelings for him.

Well, I'm not the only one with feelings. He professed his to me, too.

"My grumpy boss," I reiterate.

Ariella smiles and finishes the last of her lunch. "Right. Grumpy." She doesn't sound convinced.

"What?" I ask.

She can't deny that a man who works for the mafia isn't grumpy. It goes with the job. It's practically a requirement.

"That's not the adjective that I thought you'd have used." The smirk on her face makes me feel several degrees hotter. "You're blushing!"

I reach for my water glass, but it's empty. "He's an attractive man." There's nothing wrong with admitting that he's handsome.

His deep-set eyes and sharp jawline, his thick hair that I want to run my fingers through.

Ariella snaps her fingers in front of me. "Where'd you go?"

Oh no.

Daydreaming about Moreno.

That must be bad.

Thankfully, the waitress comes over to check on us and refills our water glasses while bringing the bill to the table. She's a welcoming distraction to shift the mood.

I grab the check, intending to pay for both of us.

"What are you doing?" Ariella holds out her hand. "At least let me pay my portion."

"You can get the bill the next time we come out." I hope there will be a next time and Moreno doesn't have a fit when he finds out I snuck out.

I shouldn't worry about what Moreno thinks. He's not my parent. I'm an adult. But I still can't let the nagging suspicion that he might be right sneak back into my head.

Ariella zips her purse. "Fine. But you're coming to dinner at my place."

"With Moreno?"

Her eyes widen. "Don't push it."

The waitress comes back to collect my credit card, and the smile disappears from my face as I glance past her and see an all too familiar face stepping into the café.

32

MORENO

"Did you have fun at the children's museum?" I ask Nova.

I'm not expecting much of an answer, but I know that she's spoken to Paige, so I at least try to engage her in conversation.

It hasn't gone as well as I'd like. But I've enjoyed spending the morning with my daughter.

Nova gives a brief nod and a slight shrug of her shoulders in response.

"What's wrong?" I ask, stopping our stroll down Maple Street.

She presses her lips together but doesn't speak. Maybe it's the fact Sawyer is with us, just a few feet away, standing guard. I made sure not to bring Bruno who had scared her with the gun incident. He's still under our employment, but he's not coming anywhere near my daughter again.

I exhale a heavy sigh. Knowing that Nova used to be a chatterbox, giggling, and full of life, it's hard.

I'm responsible for her silence.

My heart aches, and my stomach clenches, remembering the reason for her mutism.

Nova likely witnessed Laura's death. She'd been with the nanny that morning when Vance and his team broke through the gate, murdered four of my men, and breached the entrance.

Nova had been playing outside in the yard.

We had found her hidden behind the shrubs after the massacre was over.

Since that day, we've doubled the number of guards on-site at all times and installed a panic room. Is it enough?

It must be. I won't lose my daughter.

My phone buzzes in my pocket, and I grab the device and answer the caller.

"Moreno," I answer my phone.

Based on caller ID, it's Rhys, which is unusual. Dante usually calls one of the capos or me. Rhys is a soldier.

It's not that he can't contact me. It just isn't protocol.

Already, my stomach is in knots when I answer the phone.

"Boss, it's Rhys," he says. "Paige left the compound. She said that you gave her permission to leave on her own and didn't need an escort this afternoon." His voice is shaky, raspy, and filled with uncertainty.

I pinch the bridge of my nose.

Why couldn't she listen to me?

"I wasn't sure if I should call you. I apologize if I'm bothering you, sir. I just wanted to let you know in case she wasn't allowed to leave on her own. Your orders are usually that a guard escorts your daughter if she is out, but since Paige is by herself—"

I exhale a heavy sigh. "Did she take her car?"

Nova is skipping around, her floral dress flowing in the wind behind her.

"Yes, sir."

Another sigh. I only had one request, that she be escorted anywhere that she went.

Paige never listens.

Nova is getting too far ahead of me, but Sawyer is with us and keeps up with Nova to make sure that she doesn't run across the street on her own or run off.

"Thank you for letting me know," I say before ending the call.

I open the tracking app on my phone to determine Paige's most recent location. It turns out that she's not far from here.

"How about we grab some lunch?" I say to Nova, leading her toward the café a few blocks away.

Nova gives a slight shrug and a nod.

"Afterwards, we can have ice cream." I glance at her as we walk along the sidewalk.

Her smile is tight-lipped and her cheeks rosy, but the silence is deafening. I want her to talk to me again, giggle and laugh, sing songs like she used to with her mother.

While I recognize Serene is gone and those moments are in the past, I can't help but miss the little girl full of life and brightness.

Vance and the DeLucas robbed my daughter of her innocence. A four-year-old shouldn't have to witness her nanny gunned down or a funeral for her mother, all within the same week.

I groan.

Nova squeezes my hand and glances up at me.

More silence pulls at my heart. I want her to trust me, confide in me, and talk to me.

Dante and Nikki were right in pushing me to take her to a child psychologist. I shouldn't have lied, pretended Paige was my wife and everything was sunshine and rainbows.

I'm a monster.

I've hurt Nova.

Forgiveness isn't in my blood.

Is it in hers?

We cross the street, and I open the door to the café.

Paige hands her credit card to the waitress, and her gaze lands directly on me.

The smile fades from her face.

Good.

Nova spots Paige and drops my hand, rushing over to hug her.

I won't lie. It hurts that my kid lights up like a kid on Christmas morning at the first sign of Paige.

I want Nova to look at me like that, with such admiration.

Hell, I want Paige to look at me like that.

"Paige!" Nova squeals.

Damn.

Could this day get any worse?

My footsteps aren't the least bit light as I approach their table.

Nova has already climbed into the booth with Paige, making herself right at home.

Why wouldn't she? My kid adores the nanny.

Sawyer grabs a table by himself, his back to the wall so that he can watch us and the door.

"Mr. Ricci," Ariella says curtly and offers a fake smile on my approach.

The color is slowly coming back into Paige's cheeks. "Sir," she addresses me. "We were just finishing."

"Don't rush on my account," I say.

Am I the least bit pleased that she disobeyed a direct order? No, but I'm not about to make a scene at the café in front of customers, Ariella, or my daughter.

The priority is to make sure that she returns home safely with me.

Ariella glances at her phone. "I have to go pick up the kids."

I can't tell if it's a lie, or she does have to leave, but either way, it's obvious she's uncomfortable and looking for an excuse to jet out.

That's fine with me.

I wait for her to scoot out of the booth before taking her seat, situated across from Paige.

"I'll call you. Thanks for coming out today for lunch," Paige says.

Ariella leans in to hug Paige goodbye and whispers something into her ear.

I can't hear what's being said amongst the background noise of the café. Too bad.

They say their goodbyes and Ariella gives me a small wave before she dashes out the door. I don't blame her. I'm about ready to hash it out with Paige, but the only thing keeping me remotely calm is that Nova spoke.

My mouth is dry, and she's sitting with Paige, coloring on a paper placemat. Paige pulled out crayons from her purse the minute Nova sat down. Even off the clock, she's still working and always attentive to my daughter's needs.

"I know you're mad." Paige doesn't beat around the bush, and I'm appreciative of that fact with her. Unlike most people I've worked with in the past, she's direct.

"Now isn't the time to have that discussion," I say, glancing at Nova.

Paige rubs Nova's back as she scribbles mostly on the paper, but every so often, the crayon juts onto the wood table.

"Isn't that why you sat down?" Paige asks.

The waitress clears the dishes from the table, and another crew comes through, wiping and sanitizing the table.

"We came here for lunch." I stand and grab a menu along with a children's menu for Nova before returning to the table.

She presses her lips tightly together in a line. She's holding her tongue, refraining from saying something, and probably trying to decide how not to get fired. Though she did try to quit already.

I'm not letting her quit.

She's too important to Nova.

I'm also a selfish bastard and I don't want her to leave.

"I know you've already eaten, but you can have dessert. It's on me. Or if you'd prefer to return home, Sawyer can escort you back." I gesture to the guard seated across the aisle in case she hadn't noticed him.

Nova tugs on Paige's arm and gestures for her to lean down. "Stay," Nova whispers a little too loudly to be considered whispering.

"I'll need a dessert menu," Paige says to the waitress as the woman stops by the table.

"Did you have fun today with your daddy?" Paige asks. Her attention is entirely focused on my daughter.

Nova stops scribbling on the paper for a second and nods vigorously. "I missed you."

My heart aches at Nova's admission.

Paige encompasses Nova in a hug. "I missed you too, but I promise next time that you go to the children's museum, I will come with you."

"Pinky promise?" Nova holds out her pinky.

I don't want to stare, but I can't help myself. It's like I'm eavesdropping on a private moment.

Paige glances up at me with a coy smile. "On a scale of one to ten, how mad are you at me right now?"

That catches me off guard. I chuckle under my breath. "It was a ten, but seeing how good you are with Nova, it's dropped significantly." I never thought a woman could turn my ice-cold heart and warm it up.

She smiles cheekily. "Good. My plan worked."

She's teasing. I can see it in the glint in her eye.

Paige is the least manipulative person I know, but she left without a guard, which still bothers me.

It's only because I want to protect her. The thought of anything happening to her, Vance coming after Paige next because she works for the family, it makes me want to vomit.

The waitress comes by the table, and I order a sandwich for myself, mac and cheese for Nova, and Paige gets herself a slice of chocolate pie for dessert.

"So, you and Ariella are friends?" It didn't even occur to me what she might have wanted to do or who she'd have liked to visit on her day off.

While I knew they'd met at the park, I had hoped that was the end of their interaction.

Her eyes tighten. "Is that a problem?"

"No. I have no issue with Ariella." It's her husband and his band of boy scouts, the Eagle Tactical team, that rubs me the wrong way. They're not a bunch of saints like everyone thinks of them.

"Okay. Who do you have an issue with, because I'm a grown woman and can hang out with whomever I want or date whomever I want?"

Her sassy attitude has surprised me, and the comment about dating whomever she wants leaves my stomach in knots.

She isn't wrong.

Paige isn't mine.

"You're dating Ariella?" I know that's not what she means, but I want her to elaborate since she brought it up.

She snorts and rolls her eyes. "No, but you can't lock me up in your house until you feel it's safe for me to leave. By your standards, I will never be allowed outside."

That isn't true.

But she's right. I've been strict with her, but it's because I'm worried about her well-being.

"Do you have a hot date?" I need to know if she's been conversing with someone in secret. She has the entire weekend off. Is she planning on meeting up with a stranger tonight or tomorrow?

"Jealous?" she quips.

"No," I answer a little too quickly.

Nova glances up from her coloring and flips the paper over since she's colored practically every inch of the placemat.

"We should go out, just the two of us," I say.

Where the hell did that come from? I should keep my mouth shut.

She purses her lips, mulling it over. She hasn't said a word, which just makes me more nervous. I haven't dated anyone in years. The last girl I dated, I ended up marrying, Serene.

"Unless you have an aversion to dating your boss?"

Paige's face is as red as the crayon gripped tightly in Nova's fist. Is it from anger or embarrassment?

I hope she's not about to slap me for overstepping.

33

PAIGE

"I don't have an aversion to dating my boss," I say, "but I'll admit it's probably not a great idea."

He looks slightly dejected.

"But I'm not saying no," I confess. "We just need to take things slow. Okay?" I'm not even sure why he's asking me out.

He likes me, but he still seems like he's grieving for his dead wife. I don't want to be his rebound girl. Is it even a rebound after a spouse is deceased?

"Slow is good," Moreno says.

The waitress brings Nova a cup of milk in a plastic cup, with a lid and a straw, and Moreno a glass of water. She refills mine before disappearing back into the kitchen.

"I'll plan a date for just the two of us tonight."

"Tonight?" I ask and reach for my water glass.

He does move fast.

"I don't put out on a first date," I warn.

"Don't put what out?" Moreno asks innocently.

The room feels several degrees warmer, and I take another swig of my water, trying to cool down and calm down.

"You look cute when you blush."

I brush a strand of hair behind my ear. It's easier for me to focus my attention on Nova. It's why I've thrown myself into work around him and because it's also my job.

"Are you having fun coloring?" I ask Nova.

She drops her crayon and glances up at me. "You didn't answer his question. What gets put out on a date?"

My eyes widen in horror. Little Nova, who has barely spoken more than a word here or there over the past few days, has now decided it was a good time to humiliate me!

Moreno has a smug smile etched on his face. "Are you going to answer her?"

"Nova, did your daddy teach you about the birds and the bees?"

His eyes widen, and he interrupts me before I can continue any further discussion on the topic.

Moreno's ears are bright red. "Nova, sweetie, your lunch is coming out. Why don't you put the crayons down, and we go wash our hands in the bathroom?"

Wordlessly, she rests the crayon on the table and climbs out of the booth, following her father to the restroom.

I can't help but smirk, satisfied that I've managed to turn the tables on him, not that I had any intention of giving Nova the sex talk. That is up to her father to discuss when the time is appropriate. I'm her nanny, not her mother.

"Are you going to behave yourself?" Moreno asks me as he returns to the table.

I point at myself, pretending to be appalled by his suggestion. "Me?"

"Yes, you. Nova at least has the audacity to be well disciplined." Moreno's eyes are shining behind his cool exterior. There's a smirk edging at the corner of his lips. He's trying to hide it back and play the tough guy act that he wears so well.

It probably comes naturally to him.

"Yeah, I never went to finishing school or had a nanny to teach me all about the birds and the bees," I say with a chuckle.

Moreno rolls his eyes and groans.

Nova climbs onto my lap, deciding its cuddle time. "Paige, what do you mean, the birds and the bees?"

"Yes, Paige, what do you mean?" Moreno asks, tilting his head. He's trying to keep calm, but it isn't going to last at this rate. His face is red, and I think he's holding back laughter because he must know that I'm going to torture him if I can get away with it.

He doesn't seem angry, just perturbed.

Good.

That's what he gets for interrupting me when I was having lunch with Ariella earlier. Well, lunch is over, but still, payback is fair play.

The waitress brings Moreno and Nova's lunch and my dessert to the table. I gently position Nova back onto the booth beside me so that she can eat.

Nova climbs onto her knees and grabs the fork, stabbing her mac and cheese.

Thankfully, the conversation gets quickly forgotten, although I can't help but note the intentional stabbing with her fork into her food. It's almost violent as she wraps her fist around her utensil and stabs the noodle.

"Did you teach her that?" I ask, gently lifting my fork from the table as I cut into the pie. Steam wafts into the air, and I wait a few moments for it to cool off.

Moreno glances up from his sandwich and watches Nova's repeated stabbing of her macaroni.

He chuckles and wipes his face with a napkin. "No, I don't know where she learned that."

"Probably watching one of your guards." It's a joke, but he doesn't laugh.

Moreno stares at me for a long, hard second. He keeps his voice down, making sure the conversation isn't overheard by anyone else.

"We don't just randomly kill people," he says.

"I know that." I shove the fork with a bite of chocolate pie into my mouth. It's hot and burns the roof of my mouth, but I don't want to discuss his job. I realize he works for the mafia, he's killed people, and while I find all of it terrifying, I don't see the monster.

Maybe I have blinders on.

"Did she witness anyone—" I don't finish the sentence. I let it hang in the air, waiting for him to answer. What I want to know is if Nova witnessed Serene or her nanny's murder. I can't ask that question in front of Nova.

We shouldn't even be having this discussion at a café out in public.

"Likely, yes," Moreno says. "We can talk about it later. I'll tell you everything you want to know, in private."

That's as good enough of an answer for me as I'll ever get. "Thank you."

While I want to know what happened to his wife and the previous nanny, I'm not sure how I'll feel about it, either. It's obvious to me that he misses Serene. He's still in love with her. Why else would he have been so angry about her ring?

After they finish lunch and I'm done with my pie, Moreno pays the bill, and we head outside, Sawyer tagging along behind us.

It feels awkward, like we have a chaperone. Is that what it will be like when we go out on a date? He didn't bring anyone with us that night to the club.

"Daddy, ice cream," Nova says and points across the street to the ice cream shop.

"I'm going to head back to the house," I say. I've already had dessert, and while I'd love to keep them company, it's clouding up outside, and a breeze is coming in that's making me chilly.

"I promised her ice cream," Moreno says.

Grinning, I gesture to the store. "You made her a promise, and you have to keep it." I can't believe she still wants ice cream after the huge lunch she just had, but the kid would probably want it in the middle of winter too.

"Sawyer, escort her home. I'll head back with Nova after we're done getting ice cream."

I don't need a bodyguard. "That isn't necessary."

"I insist," Moreno says. His tone holds authority.

It's not that I have an issue with Sawyer. He seems like a nice enough guy, but I don't want to ride back to the cabin with him and have to chit chat. Or worse, dead, awkward silence.

"If anyone needs a second set of eyes and someone watching his back, it's you. If Nova's with you, that's where the guard needs to be." He has to see my point.

He stalls, but he doesn't look pleased. "Fine, but you're heading straight back to the house."

"Yes," I say. "I'm going to head back and take a nap."

"All right." He doesn't look pleased, but he ran into me after I snuck out. Was that a coincidence?

I doubt it.

Knowing Moreno, he has a bodyguard hidden around a tree, and I just haven't spotted him.

I wave to Nova as they dart across the street to the ice cream shop while I head in the opposite direction of my car.

Turning the corner, I shove my hand into my purse, digging out my keys, head down in front of my car.

Tires squeal, and I glance up to see a black SUV coming to an abrupt halt beside my vehicle.

Two armed men with guns leap out of the vehicle and grab me before I can run. "You're coming with us," one of them says. He's short and balding, with a huge nose.

I don't recognize him.

I don't recognize either of the men shoving me into the backseat. The other man seated in the back makes my skin crawl.

"Vance," I whisper, remembering him from our previous encounter at the club and hiring me at the agency.

"I'm glad I make a lasting impression."

34

MORENO

Paige's car is nowhere in sight. Sawyer drives us back to the compound, and I can't help but feel an overwhelming sense of dread.

Something is wrong.

I want to be overreacting, but I can't fathom why she wouldn't have returned when she explicitly said she was coming straight back to the compound.

Flinging the door open, I unbuckle Nova as she hops out of her car seat, skipping up to the front door, oblivious to my concern.

It's probably for the best.

Sawyer unlocks the front door and opens it for us.

"Head into the playroom," I say to Nova, pointing for her to go and do as I instruct.

Her shoulders slump. The skip in her step vanishes as she strolls across the hallway and into the playroom, out of sight.

"Where's Paige?" Rhys is the first guard I lay eyes on, other than Sawyer, who is with me.

"She isn't here."

"What do you mean, she isn't here?" my voice booms.

That's not an acceptable response to my question.

I stare at Rhys, expecting an answer.

"She hasn't returned, sir." Rhys looks terrified.

I want to be wrong. That I'm worried for no reason, and she's okay. But she wouldn't have gone off on another adventure without me, would she?

Pulling my phone out of my pocket, I open the tracking app, revealing that her location is turned off.

Shit.

Why is her phone off?

Where the hell is she?

Everything inside of me screams that Vance DeLuca is responsible for her disappearance. I want to be wrong. I hope I'm wrong. But I know deep down that she wouldn't run away. Not again.

———

Nikki, Luca, and Nova are locked in the panic room. We can't trust Vance won't show up with Paige as a hostage, throwing demands on us.

Standing over Dante's desk, my fingers grip the edge of the wood table. Dante stands across from me. The capos, Sawyer, Caden, and Halsey, are in the room to discuss our options.

Rhys stands guard by the front door, in case anyone shows up. He's notifying us immediately if Paige enters, or anyone else, uninvited. The guards at the post also have identical orders.

Although I suspect that we'll hear gunfire before anyone radios us.

"Do we have any idea where Vance has set up his new base?" I ask.

It's no secret that Vance moved back into town. His warning weeks ago wasn't forgotten.

Sawyer points on the map spread across the desk. "I've got surveillance putting Vance in this area, but if he's back to his old ways of trafficking women and children, his office is not going to be at the same location as the auction."

My stomach somersaults. I swallow the bile rising in my throat. I loosen my tie; the room is sweltering.

"Which means he could be holding her at one of at least two locations," Dante says. His brow is tight.

"What do you want us to do, boss?" Sawyer asks. "If we're spread too thin, we risk an ambush back here at the compound."

"That's not going to happen. This place is a fortress," Dante says. His voice holds conviction. If he has any ounce of worry or doubt, he doesn't show it.

It's part of his job, being the boss, always having to keep his shit together.

Sawyer's right, but I don't want to suggest only hitting one location. If there's an opportunity to rescue her, we need to take it.

"We'll go in with two crews and hit both locations. Our goal is to rescue Paige and take out Vance, but if we find any other girls held against their will, you have orders to get them out."

Dante isn't a saint, but he certainly looks like one compared to Vance.

Sawyer points at the nearest of the two locations, still several miles away, in the middle of nowhere. "I believe this is the location where the girls are being held for trafficking."

"I'll lead that team," I say. I can't stand around and wait to hear what happens to Paige. She means too much to me, and if Vance hasn't killed her yet, I can only surmise that he intends to sell her to the highest bidder.

She's not just a nanny. She's done so much for my daughter and my family. The least I can do is try to free her from the enemy.

"Good," Dante says. "I'll hit the location of the auction. It's less likely she'll be there. She hasn't been gone but a few hours, and they tend to break the girls mentally before selling them."

The images of Paige being forced to do things for random men blur my vision. I storm out of the office, unable to breathe.

I stumble through the hallway and open the front door, barely making it down the step and onto the grass. The air doesn't cool me down fast enough. I bend over, sick.

Weakness.

I must get my shit together if I'm going on a mission to save Paige and take down DeLuca's men.

The nausea is gone as fast as it surfaced and is now replaced with infuriating heat and rage. I storm inside, slamming the door.

Rhys jumps out of the way, startled.

In a blaze, I'm back in Dante's office. "Let's armor up," I say.

I don't want to waste another minute talking. We have a plan. We know where we're going and who is on what team. We have radios to communicate with each other with whatever we find.

Good or bad.

"Dismissed," Dante says and waves the capos out of the room. "Moreno, a word."

Sawyer shuts the door on the way out, leaving Dante and me alone.

"Yes, boss."

"Don't let Vance get inside your head," he warns.

I snort under my breath. Vance is always in there, the realization that he murdered my wife, stole my daughter's mother away, and destroyed my family.

Now he's taken Paige.

"It's too late for that, sir." I'm far from having a level head. The minute I see Vance, I'm taking the kill shot.

35

PAIGE

"Nice of you to join us," Vance says.

The door slams shut behind me. I try the handle, but it's child-safety locked.

Why would I expect anything less from men like Vance?

"Like I had a choice in the matter." His goons pulled me off the street at gunpoint and thrust me into the back of the SUV.

The driver jets off, away from the small downtown area of Breckenridge.

Vance snatches my purse, rolls down the window, and tosses it out the window.

"Hey!" I squeal.

"Your phone can be tracked," Vance says.

He could have just pulled out my phone, but he chose to dump my entire purse, wallet, and inside contents on the street to get run over by the next passing vehicle.

Jerk.

"What do you want with me?" I ask. If he plans on killing me, would he have even bothered to nab me off the street first?

I still don't know what happened to Serene or Laura. Were they tortured before they died?

A shiver runs through my body.

Did he murder them or have his goons do it? Could Moreno be mistaken?

Vance reaches his hand out to stroke my cheek. "I just want to have a little fun. Don't worry, princess."

I pull back. There's nowhere for me to go.

"I'm not your princess," I snarl at him. He'd better keep his grubby paws off me.

My back is against the window of the SUV. The door handle doesn't open. I can try rolling down the window and throwing myself through the open pane, but the driver picks up speed, and I doubt I'll get more than halfway out before Vance grabs me and drags me back inside.

And that assumes that I can open the window.

As we travel farther from Breckenridge, there are fewer vehicles on the road.

I should have heeded Moreno's warning and taken Sawyer with me. At least then, I'd have had a fighting chance.

But what if Vance would have gone after Moreno and Nova if Sawyer had been protecting me?

Vance leans in and every hair on my body stands on end.

A warning that my life is in danger.

No kidding.

My heart is pounding against my ribcage, reminding me that I'm trapped, but eventually, the vehicle will have to come to a stop, and when someone opens the back door, I'll run.

"I like a little bite in a girl," Vance says. He doesn't smile. I doubt he's ever grinned in his life.

He grabs a fistful of my hair and brings my face closer.

I swallow back my fear. I won't cower to him. He probably likes watching women beg for their lives.

"What do you want with me?" I ask him for the second time.

"Smart and pretty. A rare combination," Vance says. "I have a proposition for you."

"No." My answer comes before I can even hear or think about his offer. Whatever it is, it won't be good.

"No one tells Don DeLuca no." Vance grabs my neck and pulls me close enough to kiss me.

My breathing hitches out of fear. His breath is putrid. His body odor burns my nostrils. His scent makes me want to hurl.

If he tries to kiss me, I'll bite his mouth.

"I intend to take down Moreno, and I want your help. You will help me, princess."

Is he out of his mind? "Why would I ever help you?"

He must be crazy to think that I'm going to betray Moreno.

"Because if you don't, I'll come after the little girl, rape her, kill her, and Moreno will never forgive you when he finds out it's all your fault. You've been working for me since the beginning. Remember?"

"You're a monster," I seethe between gritted teeth.

Vance drops his hold on me, but I feel as though I'm suffocating in the back of the vehicle.

Moreno wouldn't blame me. Would he? I should have come clean about the agency, that Vance was running the operation.

But I can't let him hurt Nova.

"You won't touch her," I say. "Only a coward would harm a child, let alone threaten one."

Vance backhands me across the face. "Careful who you're calling names, princess."

The sting burns and brings tears to my eyes. I don't want to cry, especially not in front of him, but the pain is as overwhelming as the emotional trauma of his words.

Picturing Nova screaming for help, begging for Vance to let her go, is terrifying to me.

I can't let anything happen to Nova.

"If you so much as harm a hair on that child's head, I'll kill you myself."

Vance and the other men in the vehicle laugh at my threat.

"I won't touch her if you do exactly as I say."

I'm afraid to ask what he wants me to do. While I'd never want to hurt Moreno, I also can't let anything happen to Nova. I'd never be able to live with myself if he so much as harmed a hair on that child's head.

Vance takes my silence as acceptance.

Whatever he wants of me, it will involve betrayal.

Moreno will never forgive me.

———

He doesn't tell me his plan, what he expects me to do to help him. I'm waiting for the anchor weighing down my stomach to disappear.

At this rate, it never will. I'm drowning and Vance is going to take me down with him.

I glance out the side window, recognizing the route that we're taking. It's a back road through the forest, and if I'm not mistaken, it's only a few miles from the cabin where I've been staying with the Ricci family.

The SUV pulls to an abrupt halt.

"One of our men is on the inside, working for us." Vance stares at me grimly. "He'll be watching you."

I'm not sure whether to believe him or not.

There's been no evidence of anyone working for Vance except for my abduction. Is it possible he knew that I was alone today? But then why grab me after lunch and not before?

I'll have to tread carefully.

"Your employer won't be around much longer. Let's just say the smoke will be getting to him."

Is this a game for him? A riddle? Is he talking about the fire that Nova set or another forthcoming fire?

Bile rises to my throat. "What do you expect of me?" I ask.

He wants me to do something. He's not telling me this out of the goodness of his heart. I doubt the man has anything more than a heart of stone.

"If you want to save that little girl, you'd better get far away fast."

He wants me to take the child from her home?

Is he crazy?

"Boom!" he shouts, his hands in fists and then opening fast like an explosion. "The Riccis will burn, along with everyone inside."

The door clicks to the vehicle. My heart is pounding wildly in my chest. I open the car door and bolt out before they can grab me.

Are they letting me go?

I don't look back over my shoulder as I tear into the forest to escape.

All I hear is thick, deep laughter and shouts. "Run, princess!"

36

MORENO

I lead the team, with Sawyer, Caden, and six additional soldiers behind me. We don't have active surveillance or audio.

It's risky, going in blind, but we must find Paige.

I won't let anything happen to her.

The walkie-talkie is attached to my belt loop. There's been only radio silence.

My cell phone hasn't buzzed, either.

While the signal is strong at our current location and there's a nearby cell tower, there's been no response, which means no news.

Paige is still unaccounted for. She's out there, being held by Vance against her will. I can only fathom all the terrible acts that he's doing to her, and it makes my stomach flop.

If he wanted her dead, he wouldn't have been shy and would have murdered her in broad daylight, just like he did my wife, Serene.

Vance is a monster. Coming after what matters most to me, family.

Why me? Why my family? Not that I want anything to happen to Luca or Nikki, but his fascination with torturing me needs to end.

We take out the guards first, at the entrance of their hideaway. Two guards versus nine of us, there's no issue breaking in through the main gates, though we are overzealous with bullets, shooting several rounds into each guard.

Once we're through the gate, we rush for the main door to the brick building. This isn't where they used to house the girls. It's newly built but lacks the level of security that one might expect for a trafficking operation.

Where are the additional guards on the perimeter?

"Keep moving," I order my men to head inside the facility. Time isn't on our side.

The eruption of gunfire had to be noticed. Their men are likely getting armed and prepared for us.

Caden shoots the handle of the door, granting us entrance inside. He and two of his soldiers enter first, sweeping the area, shooting anyone deemed a threat.

Female screams echo from down below.

The floorboards squeak and wheeze, bouncing as we walk. Each step hallow. It's obvious there's a basement, a bunker, some type of underground prison below.

We haven't found the door for it yet.

There are too many of Vance's men with guns shooting at us as we fire back.

A blaze of gunfire cracks one right after the other.

Blood spews as we take out four men.

Four.

It's too few to be guarding a compound of this magnitude.

Female voices scream and shout down below our feet.

"Paige!" I don't recognize her voice amongst the women crying for help, begging for safety and freedom.

I kick a gun away from one of the dead men.

"Something's off," I say, glancing at Sawyer.

Caden bounces on the floorboards that have too much give. He stoops down and pries open one of the wooden slats.

"Hello?" Caden bends farther down and calls to where the sound of voices echoed for help.

I lean down and pull two more boards with him. "Give us a hand!"

Sawyer and another soldier work the boards loose, one by one, to find four women trapped in the darkness, covered in dirt and filth.

"Paige?" I don't see any sign of her.

"Sir," a younger guard, Giovanni, says. His voice holds a hint of a quiver.

"What is it?" I don't so much as look over my shoulder. We rip the last of the floorboards away to lift the girls out from their prison.

We don't have time to dick around. At any moment, more reinforcements could be on their way, and we still have to locate Paige.

"There's a bomb."

My stomach knots. None of us know a damn thing about disassembling a bomb. "Is it on a timer?" I ask Giovanni.

My attention remains on the blonde under the floorboards. I lie down on the wood floor and hold out my arms, pulling her up. Sawyer does the same to help the youngest girl who can't be more than twelve.

What the fuck is wrong with Vance?

Why would he take a child from her home?

I know the answer, and bile rises to my throat just thinking about the monster that he is, selling women and children to marry off.

It's disgusting.

"Yes. There's a minute and thirty-five seconds, sir." He starts counting down.

Caden yanks another girl, in her early twenties, from beneath the ground.

There's one girl left.

"Get out of here!" I demand.

The little girl just stands there, shivering in shock. Sawyer lifts her and carries her out the front door.

"Give me your hand." I won't leave the last girl behind. It doesn't matter that we're running out of time.

"I can't. Save yourself," she says.

I plop back down on the floor and extend my reach, stretching my arms down to help lift her out. It's clear her arm is already dislocated, and that's why she's hesitant to use her arm to let me lift her.

It's a struggle to pull her up, not to mention the bomb just a few feet away.

The moment I have her lifted, we barrel out the same way I came in, heading for the open door.

Boom!

37

PAIGE

I tear through the forest in haste. I'm not the least bit careful. Branches scrape against my arms and legs. I ignore the sting. It's nothing compared to my pulse pounding so loud that I think I may go deaf.

There's noise in the distance behind me.

Vance's men are gaining on me.

Their voices are muffled, but they're tracking me.

Why did they let me go if they only intended to hunt me down? Is this a game to Vance? Let me think I've won my freedom, only to snatch it right back?

What did they mean, *boom*?

Dozens of questions rattle through my head as I keep heading through the forest and refuse to slow my pace.

Did they plant a bomb? If they did, I need to warn Moreno and the others. But who is working with the DeLucas?

I don't know the guards well enough to determine if any of them would betray Moreno. Dante would never be the rat. He's the boss and married to Nikki. I can't fathom that she would be working for Vance, although she was part of their family.

At least at one time.

Was she playing Dante and Moreno?

While I doubt it, I also can't take the chance that she or anyone else will hurt Nova.

The bottoms of my feet throb as I approach the metal fence around the perimeter. I'm not at the gate, so I hurry and follow the fence around until I reach the guard post at the entrance.

I'm out of breath—my heart hammering in my chest.

"Paige," Leone's voice is like music to my ears.

Safety.

Security.

Protection.

I need to get to Nova to protect her and warn the others about Vance.

"I need to talk to Moreno," I say. I must look as dirty and disgusting as I feel. I'm coated in sweat from running. My feet hurt, my skin is scraped and bloody.

Leone unlocks the gate, and the metal doors squeak as they open.

"Vance isn't far behind," I warn the guard. "I escaped and ran through the forest, but I'm sure they were following me. Some of the men were on foot, others were in a black SUV."

They didn't snatch me from town to give me a joy ride and threaten the family. There's more to Vance. He's a murderer and a monster.

"Get inside," Leone says and points at the cabin.

"Where's Nova?" Is she all right?

"Nova is in the panic room with Nikki and Luca. You should get in there yourself. Go!" Leone shouts.

He's doesn't seem happy that I'm standing there asking questions when I've told him Vance and the others are on their way.

I hurry inside the building. Leone radios someone on his walkie-talkie, but I can't hear what's being said.

I'm a mess, and ordinarily I'd take off my shoes before entering the cabin, especially after trampling through the forest, but my main concern right now is Nova.

If what Vance alluded to was true and there's a bomb somewhere in the home, I can't let anything happen to Nova.

I tear up the stairs to the panic room.

I don't have the code. "Nikki!" I know where the door is and knock repeatedly. She can see me from a camera if she wants to make sure that I'm alone.

The lock clicks and the door opens slowly. Nikki unlocked it for me.

She trusts me.

Why wouldn't she?

"Is it over?" Nikki asks, glancing me up and down, her brow furrowed at my appearance.

I storm into the panic room, and Nova rushes right toward me, throwing her arms around me as I bend down to lift her.

"I have to go," I say, carrying Nova out of the panic room and down the hallway.

"Where are you going? Where's Moreno and Dante? Are they back yet?" Nikki asks.

Bruno, one of the guards I'm least familiar with, lands eyes on Nova and me. I'm cautious with my words. What if he works for Vance?

I can't warn Nikki. I can only hope that she returns to the panic room and it's fireproof.

"They're on their way back," I say. It's an easy lie. She helped set it up by telling me they're gone.

I have no clue when either of the men are returning. I assume they're trying to help locate me, but Vance seems to be one step ahead of us.

I hurry down the stairwell to the door.

"Where are you taking Nova?" Nikki asks. Her tone is much more insistent.

"I have to get her someplace safe. Go back in the panic room," I instruct.

"But you said Dante and Moreno are on their way back. How did you get here—" Nikki's eyes widen, and she grabs Luca, shoving him behind her as the front door swings open.

"Paige, Nikki," Vance says with a cunning smile. "It's so nice to see you both again." He holds the door open and gestures for me to take Nova outside.

I grab the keys sitting by the door. It's not my car, mine's still in town, but I'll take whatever I can get my hands on that starts.

I hit the unlock button and the SUV a few yards down flashes the headlights when I unlock the vehicle. I hurry with Nova, opening the backdoor.

There's no car seat.

Well, this is an emergency. I strap her into the middle seat and pray that I don't end up in an accident.

I slam the door shut and hurry around to the front, hopping inside the driver's seat. I start the engine and put the SUV into reverse, flooring it. Turning the vehicle around, I glide the gear into drive and head for the main gates.

Will Leone let me pass through the main entrance?

As I approach, the guard gates are wide open, the guard tower empty.

Where's Leone?

Is he dead?

Does he work for Vance? Is that how Vance was able to bypass security?

A shudder runs through my body.

I hit the gas and refuse to look back.

"Where are we going?" Nova asks.

It's the first time that I miss her silence.

38

MORENO

My ears ring.

Everything aches.

But I'm still alive.

The shockwave slams us against the ground. The heat of the fire blasts behind us from the explosion as the building becomes nothing but ash.

"Paige," I whisper.

Where is she?

I should be relieved she wasn't in the building, but we didn't have time to search every room or floor from top to bottom before the explosion. We were focused on rescuing the girls, screaming for help.

My radio is fried. My phone is dead.

The explosion killed my equipment, but Sawyer's phone appears to be working. He's communicating with someone, but all I hear is ringing in my ears.

I feel like I'm screaming when I speak.

"Paige?"

I need to know that she's all right.

He's nodding slowly, and I can see him mouthing the word 'yes,' but that's all I can make out.

———

We took three vehicles on our mission. The soldiers rode together in one SUV.

Sawyer rides back with the girls, dropping them off at the police station. We want to get them help but also don't want to get any further involved and have the police ask us questions.

Caden and I head straight back to the compound.

Paige is there.

Or was there?

I can't make sense of what was said, only that I need to return immediately.

My stomach sinks as we near. The gate is wide open.

Leone was manning the gate. Why the hell isn't it shut? Where the hell is he?

The booth is empty. There's no sign of him, only a smear of blood.

"This doesn't look good," Caden says.

No shit.

There are three vehicles that I don't recognize parked in front of our compound.

Vance and his men.

It's the only explanation that makes sense. He led us away to conquer our home, our castle.

Is he after Nikki? Luca?

He already nabbed Paige, but she was back at the compound. That's what the message that was delivered to us said.

Unless they lied and wanted us to return.

"Give me your phone." We need to get ahold of Dante. I don't see his vehicle, which means that he's not back yet.

Vance had set up a trap for us with the bomb. Who knows what danger Dante might have walked into at the location of the auction.

Would they have set off a second bomb?

———

Caden manages to get ahold of Dante. He's already on his way back to the compound with Rhys, Halsey, and several soldiers who accompanied them.

In a matter of minutes, Dante is pulling in through the gates just behind us. We're standing outside, grabbing weapons from the trunk, ensuring that we're fully armed and prepared for whatever lies ahead of us.

We storm inside the compound through the front door.

Dante leads the assault. Together, the two of us take out several guards on entering the premises. Sawyer and Caden are right on our heels, watching our backs as we stretch on through the hallway.

The firefight is just beginning.

From within the office, Vance's gravelly voice carries through the hallway.

Our soldiers secure the remainder of the house. Dante, Sawyer, Rhys, and I head in for the office.

Dante leads, and I'm right on his heel.

"Well, well, well," Vance says. He sits with his feet up on Dante's desk, reclining in the leather chair. "Look who decided to finally pay us a visit."

There are two guards immediately inside the door, Marco and Rafael, and four more behind Vance I don't recognize.

"Guns on the floor, boys," Vance says.

"This is my home. Get your feet off my damn desk and your ass out of my chair," Dante snaps.

My gun is drawn, aimed at Vance. I know the minute I pull the trigger, it'll be a blood bath.

Vance removes his feet from the desk but doesn't get up from his seat. "That's no way to talk to guests."

"You're not a guest. You're vermin," I say.

Why is he here? What does he want?

"You'll never touch Nikki," Dante says. He keeps his gun trained on Vance.

"Do you think I want her anymore? Her father is dead. If she had been around, I'd have had to fight her for the throne," Vance says. "Instead, the family is mine, and I control all of it." He collapses his hands together on the desk.

"Why are you here? Where's Paige?" It takes everything in me not to lunge at him and wrap my hands around his neck and strangle the life right out of him.

"Paige left with your daughter," Vance says with a wry grin. "She kidnapped your little star."

I swallow the lump in my throat.

He's lying.

Paige would never kidnap Nova.

"What do you want?" I seethe between gritted teeth.

"Nothing more than to see you suffer." Vance takes pleasure in my pain.

I want to pretend it doesn't bother me, but Nova is my flesh and blood, my kin. Abandoning her isn't in my DNA. "Why?" I ask.

Anger seeps through me, and I stomp in past the guards, shoving the barrel of my gun under Vance's chin, pointing it upward.

All he's ever done is cause me pain.

Two men are on me, one pistol on my back, the other at my head. None of it matters.

I need answers. "Why did you murder my wife?"

"Drop the gun, Moreno," Rafael says.

I ignore him. "Answer me!" I demand Vance.

"Serene worked for me. I hired her to infiltrate your family, destroy you from the inside. I paid her to marry you." The smug look on his face boils my blood.

Lies.

"I don't believe you." What is he going to say next, that he hired Paige to pretend to be a nanny?

"I killed Serene because she was supposed to abandon you and bring me Nova. When she refused, I shot her nanny as a warning, and when she didn't come with me, I took care of the problem. I don't want your brat. I only wanted to hurt you. Good thing Paige is a good listener."

"Get out of my house," Dante seethes.

Gunfire erupts upstairs.

Vance doesn't so much as blink at the sound. Whether it's his men under fire or doing the killing, it doesn't seem to faze him.

"You'd better put that away," Vance says, referring to the gun poised under his chin. "Assuming you want to see your daughter again."

"Where's Nova?"

"You don't listen," Vance says. "I told you, she's with Paige, far away from here." His eyes twinkle with mirth.

I swallow the bile that rises in my throat.

No.

He's lying.

"Get out of my house!" Dante's voice echoes throughout the room.

Vance holds up his hands in mock surrender and slowly stands.

It's all mind games to him, manipulation, fucking with us any way he can to torture us. It takes everything inside of me to lower the gun and not shoot him in cold blood.

He murdered Serene but if I kill him, I may never see my daughter.

39

PAIGE

"Where's Daddy?" Nova asks. She continues with the questions, buckled into the backseat, bouncing around, not wanting to sit still.

I don't blame her. The girl has been through a lot in such a short time.

I need to protect Nova, but I'm not sure how. Going on the run seems a dangerous idea. I'm not trying to kidnap Moreno's daughter.

I want to protect her.

The only way I know how is to hide in plain sight.

I don't have my phone, but I remember the address that Ariella gave me and the location of her house.

Pulling up in the driveway, I shut off the engine and open the back door to help Nova out of the SUV.

"Where are we?" Nova asks.

I haven't answered her questions. I don't know how to without scaring her. "We're going for a surprise playdate," I say. "Do you remember Ariella from lunch?"

Nova nods and clutches my hand.

I'm grimy and covered in filth. I need a shower, but none of that matters right now. I knock forcefully on the front door and wait for someone to answer.

Hopefully, Ariella is home. There was a car out front.

The lock clicks and slides and a moment later, she's pulling the door open, staring at me.

"Are you okay?" Ariella asks.

One look at me, and she can sense danger.

"Who's at the door?" Jaxson's voice carries from the kitchen to the foyer.

"Come in," Ariella says, ushering us into the house. She glances past us, obviously looking for whatever danger must be following us. She locks the door behind us and arms the alarm.

"Thank you," I say.

"Jaxson, it's the new nanny I was telling you I befriended at the park, Paige."

Jaxson shuts off the sink in the kitchen and hurries over to greet us.

"Paige," he says, glancing me up and down.

"I promise I won't stay long. I just need somewhere to keep Nova safe."

"The police station is usually the proper place. If something happened with Moreno or the family and your life is in danger—"

"It's nothing like that," I say and hold up my hand. "Maybe we should have this discussion in private." I don't want to scare Nova any more than she already has been after what's happened today.

Jaxson gives a firm nod. "Good idea. Ariella will keep an eye on Nova and get her something to eat while we have a little chat."

He gestures me to follow him through the kitchen toward a back bedroom.

Jaxson shuts the door behind me with a loud thump.

I jump from the sound. I'm still on edge after everything that's transpired today.

"Ariella already told me that you're working for the Riccis."

I had assumed that much when he brought up Moreno. "Yes, but they're not the problem. Are you familiar with a man by the name of Vance DeLuca?" I exhale a heavy sigh.

My chest is heavy. Everything inside of me hurts.

Just being out of Nova's sight, has me worked up into a frenzy, but I trust Ariella with her.

"I know of him," Jaxson says. He folds his arms across his chest. "What's going on, Paige?"

"Vance grabbed me off the street this afternoon when I was heading to my car. He kidnapped me, threatened me, and told me that if I didn't help him, he'd hurt Nova. Then he made this sound like he was hinting to me that he was going to blow up the Ricci household, and so I grabbed Nova to protect her."

Jaxson's face is firm.

I can't tell if he believes me or thinks that I'm mad.

"I can't let anything happen to that little girl," I plead with him to help me. He has to understand. He's a father.

"And you told Moreno that you took his daughter?" Jaxson asks. His tone is calm, but I can see the cogs going in his head.

"Well, no. He wasn't home. And I couldn't leave a note. Vance broke in the minute I managed to get downstairs with Nova. It looks bad, and I get it. Nikki probably thinks I kidnapped Nova."

"You did kidnap her." Jaxson pinches the bridge of his nose.

"No, it wasn't like that." He has to see this from my point of view, Nova's life was in danger, and I was doing everything that I possibly could to protect her by taking her out of that house and saving her from an explosion that Vance intends to set off.

"Moreno is going to come looking for you."

I'd expect nothing less from him. He loves his daughter, and he won't stop until he finds her.

"I know, and that's why I need you to keep her safe. If I stay, I don't know what he'll do to me."

The words rattle through my head, *mafia prince*, and a shudder runs down my spine.

Moreno has never hurt me, but if he thinks I betrayed him, my life is in further danger.

40

MORENO

My heart pounds hard against my ribcage. It feels like it might burst through my chest as sweat coats my forehead.

"Where's Nova?" I need to see my daughter and know that she's safe.

Vance is full of lies. Paige would never work for him.

Dante shouts orders for the capos and soldiers to clean up the bodies and secure the compound.

Nikki is coming down the stairs with Luca at her side. Dante already let them know it was safe to reemerge and that I would have questions for her.

I rush across the hallway.

"Where's Nova?" I had secured her in the panic room with Nikki and Luca before leaving.

How did she get out?

"I'm so sorry," Nikki's voice trembles. "Paige came, and I opened the door. I shouldn't have, but I thought you were both back, and it was all over." Guilt weighs heavily on her features.

It's pale compared to the devastation that I feel.

I will not lose my daughter.

"Where did she take her, Nikki?" I'm not the least bit calm or rational right now.

I need answers.

"I don't know. Vance came in and let her leave. She's working with him!"

I can't believe that, but after what Vance said about Serene, my head is in a whirlwind. I don't know what to believe anymore or who to trust.

But I need my daughter. Her safety is my number one priority. "How'd she leave?" I ask.

Her vehicle was still in town, abandoned when she'd been abducted.

"I don't know. She grabbed a set of car keys," Nikki says.

I hurry outside to take note of what vehicles are still missing. "She took the SUV. Dante, I need your phone." I don't bother to explain, only to interrupt him.

"Why can't you use yours?" he asks, pulling out his cell phone and unlocks it before handing it to me.

"It got fried in the explosion," I say. I open the tracking app and pull up the specific vehicle that she nabbed.

Sure enough, the GPS is ticking on the map, indicating that she hasn't left town.

I grab the keys and rush out the door.

Nikki chases after me. "Do you need backup?"

I doubt she's offering to help, other than inform the soldiers that I want an escort.

"No, I've got it." I don't want to spook Paige.

If there's any chance that she's working for Vance, I need to know, and bringing an army could only cause more trouble.

Besides, by the looks of where she's going, we'll be starting a war if I bring soldiers. We need to keep off the radar.

41

PAIGE

"Do you plan on running?" Jaxson asks.

"What other choice do I have? I worked for Vance! Moreno will never forgive me, and as long as Vance is alive, I'll always be a pawn to him, a tool he can use to hurt Moreno. Next time, he may not let me go, and I've heard he murdered Serene and Laura. I won't be next."

While I'm not sure whether he specifically murdered Serene and Laura or his men did, he's still fully responsible for their deaths.

Jaxson presses his lips together. "Might I make a suggestion?"

I fold my arms defensively across my chest. "What?"

"Talk to Moreno before you leave."

I don't want to admit to Jaxson or anyone that I'm afraid of how Moreno will react when he finds me.

"That's not a good idea," I say as I shuffle toward the door. The sooner I leave, the farther I can get before he shows up looking for Nova.

Coming to Ariella and Jaxson's home was the first place I thought to go, which means Moreno will have the same idea. It's no secret that Ariella and I have become friends.

"We've got company!" Ariella calls from the living room.

I haven't heard the door yet. Maybe she's looking out the window?

"Stay here," Jaxson instructs as he heads out of the bedroom and shuts the door behind himself.

I hurry toward the window in the bedroom and glance through the blinds.

My stomach is in knots as I catch sight of Moreno stepping out of his SUV. I think I'm going to be sick.

Scratch that. I know I'm going to be sick.

I want to run.

Maybe I should.

Moreno heads to the front door, and I open the window and climb out, making a beeline for the SUV I borrowed earlier.

I dig the keys out of my pocket and jump into the vehicle, hitting the start button for the engine. I put the SUV in drive, and the front door of Ariella's home flings open.

Moreno stands there, watching me as I slam on the gas.

All I see in his gaze is disappointment.

And maybe anger mixed in.

He's not happy to see me. Why would I expect him to be?

My tires squeal, and Moreno removes his gun from his hip and points it at the car as he approaches.

He's not really going to shoot me.

Is he?

He fires several rounds at the ground, blowing the tires before I can leave the driveway.

I slam my fist on the steering wheel.

Moreno gestures for me to get out of the vehicle.

Is he going to shoot me?

"Do you have a set of handcuffs on you?" he shouts at Jaxson.

I didn't even bother to lock the car door when I rushed inside.

Moreno yanks the handle of the car open, his gun trained on me. I don't know how many bullets he has left, but I don't want to find out.

"Are you going to have me arrested?" I ask.

Is that why he's insisting on having me handcuffed? Is he going to haul my ass off to jail? Will he call the cops and turn me in for kidnapping Nova and stealing his vehicle?

"No," Moreno says.

Jaxson is beside him in no time, handing over a set of metal cuffs.

Moreno yanks me out of the car, forcing my hands behind my back as he presses me against the SUV.

I feel the cold metal clasp against my wrists.

"What do you plan on doing?" I'm not sure that I want to know what will happen, but I find the need to ask anyhow.

"You'll find out soon enough." He opens the passenger door to his vehicle and shoves me inside.

Moreno grabs the seatbelt and leans across my body, snapping the buckle into place before slamming the door shut.

Ariella steps outside, carrying Nova. She gives me an apologetic look, like she feels guilty for betraying me.

She shouldn't.

I did this to myself.

Betraying Moreno was a choice I made to save Nova. I'd do it all over again.

It's time I live with the consequences.

42

MORENO

"Nikki, can you put Nova to bed?" I ask, heading inside the compound.

Nova has been silent. Not that I expected much out of her.

Paige seems to have taken a lesson from Nova.

"Sure. Come on," Nikki says and leads her up the stairs.

I wait for her to disappear down the hallway before I return to the SUV and escort Paige out of the vehicle in handcuffs.

"Are the cuffs really necessary?" It's the first thing she's said to me since I got into the vehicle with her.

No apology.

No explanation.

Just silence.

"Until I have answers and can trust you again, yes." I yank her inside the house, my hand gripping her arm as I lead her down to the holding cells.

"Where are we going?" her voice cracks.

This time, I respond in silence. I hit the light switch and the lights flicker on as we descend the stairwell into the basement.

Several prison cells are lined up in the basement with iron bars and no windows. The walls are made of cement, and the room is quite chilly, even for summer.

I open the cell door and thrust her inside. "Turn around," I instruct and unlock the cuffs, letting her hands free.

I pocket the handcuffs and shut the prison door, locking her inside before turning for the stairwell.

"Moreno," she says, her voice sounding broken. How do I know it's not just another game to her? "Please, let me explain."

I storm up the stairs. I need to tuck Nova into bed and see how my little girl is doing after the day she's endured.

Once Nova is asleep, I'll pay another visit to Paige, but for now, I'd rather make her wait and wonder when I'll be back for her.

The prison cell is absent of a bed. There's a bucket to piss in. There are no blankets, no warm comforts, not even a chair. Although from time to time, we bring one in and let the prisoner sit while we tie them up and torture the bastards.

I trudge up the stairs, leaving the prison lights on.

I shut the basement door and head down the hallway and up the stairs to check on Nova.

Nikki is just stepping out of Nova's bedroom. "She's changed for bed and tucked in. She doesn't seem tired, but she rolled over and pretended to be asleep when I offered to read her a bedtime story."

"Thanks, Nikki." I appreciate the help.

Nikki stands tall, staring up at me. She doesn't seem to take a clue that she's dismissed.

"Why did you bring Paige back here, under our roof? She kidnapped your daughter." Nikki waits for me to respond.

If she did kidnap Nova, she did a terrible job by bringing her to Ariella and Jaxson's home. And Paige wouldn't have willingly gone with Vance earlier in the afternoon. I can't let the nagging suspicion that she'd been set up just like I had, with the explosion at the facility where we infiltrated.

"I don't have to explain myself to you," I say.

Nikki scoffs. "Well, you'll have to explain yourself to Dante." She storms down the hallway, her heels clicking forcefully against the floorboards.

Is she trying to wake Nova? She certainly is causing a scene.

Several guards glance in our direction as Nikki thunders down the stairs.

Exhaling a sigh, I head into Nova's bedroom to tuck my little girl into bed. Except for her unicorn nightlight beside the bed, the lights are off.

She rolls around and peeks out through heavy lids, sitting up in bed the minute she sees me. "Where's Paige?" Nova asks.

"She can't tuck you into tonight."

The pout on her bottom lip makes my stomach flop. The girl is in love with her nanny.

Yeah, well, so am I.

Now I'm eternally conflicted.

"Do you want to tell me what happened today?" I ask. I trust Nova's narrative of events, whatever they might be.

Nova plops back on the mattress and pulls the covers up around herself. She shuts her eyes.

That's a no.

I sit at the edge of Nova's bed, hoping to get her to talk to me and open up. "Did Paige tell you where she was taking you?"

Again, I'm met with silence.

"Nova, I need to know what happened, or I'm going to have to send Paige away."

"No!" she squeals and sits up in bed, her eyes wide and her forehead sweaty. It's like she had a bad dream, but it's all too real.

I'm not sure what I'm expecting from a four-year-old. Maybe I'm giving Nova too much credit to explain what happened and defend Paige or implicate her.

————

I thunder down the stairs to the prison.

Nova is tucked into bed, and I can't stand still long enough to grab something to eat, let alone a glass of water. At this rate, I'd throw it against the wall out of frustration.

Paige owes me an explanation.

I demand answers.

"How long have you been working for Vance DeLuca?" There are no pleasantries on my approach.

She's seated on the floor. It's cold and dusty. Paige doesn't even attempt to stand when I storm down the steps into the basement.

"He runs the nanny agency that you hired. I had no idea who he was, the connection to your family, any of it until the night at the club when he showed up. I'm not loyal to him," she says.

Paige stares up at me. She doesn't stand or move from her position on the floor.

I watch her expression and try to read her eyes, whether she flinches or not. I study her lips and if her voice quivers when she speaks.

I've interrogated dozens of men in these very cells and tortured most of them.

I recognize no signs of her lying to me, but that doesn't mean she doesn't have me fooled. Serene certainly did if what Vance said was true.

"And when he showed up at the club, and after I told you about Serene, you still didn't come clean!"

"I'm sorry," she whispers, staring right at me. "I was afraid."

The anger builds inside of me. "So, you thought you'd snatch my daughter and take her, what, for a joy ride up to Jaxson's place?"

Paige lets out a heavy sigh. "That isn't what happened."

"Then give me your side, Paige. I'm dying to hear what made you kidnap my daughter," I snap.

She grimaces, and her eyes crinkle at my words.

"Vance and his men forced me into their vehicle this afternoon."

That fits the story that I know and why she didn't come home, but I can't help but doubt her words. "Forced, or you went willingly? You do work for him."

"They held me at gunpoint," she says.

"And?" I need more out of her.

She's hesitating. Her eyes twitch, and she shifts uncomfortably on the floor, unfolding her legs and then pulling them up to her chest.

"And nothing. You want to lock me in here. I deserve it. I was played," Paige says. She rests her chin on her knees. "I was stupid enough to walk through that front door at the agency and request a job. I believed Vance's threats were real. There probably wasn't a traitor in your house or a bomb set up to go off. He played me."

"It was stupid to listen to him," I say, but the anger that I harbor slowly begins to dissipate. "There was a bomb, but it wasn't here."

"What?" Her eyes widen in clear shock. She had no idea what I'd been through. One glance over her filthy and torn clothes, the red marks and dried scrapes of blood, and I don't know what she went through, either.

"DeLuca tried to kill my men and me," I say. "Dante's lucky he wasn't nearly blown to pieces too." I run a hand through my hair.

I can still feel the wave of the blast and the heat that threw me down to the ground.

My men would never betray me. They know the cost, their lives.

"Are you still working for Vance DeLuca?" I ask again.

I need to know without a doubt that Paige is loyal to the Ricci family and me.

Her eyes are wide and bright as she stares up at me. "My only connection to him was the nanny agency, and you provide me my paycheck. I don't have any further ties to him."

She's right. I paid Nanny Agency, Inc. handsomely for hiring Paige. I had no idea who I was funding.

I believe her, but it still doesn't take away the anger and pain, the betrayal that burns inside me.

"Does he call you? Text you?" I ask.

"No. He kidnapped me off the street and had his men chase me through the forest. I swear I haven't been in contact with him since I walked into his office and requested a job."

It's all a game to Vance.

Manipulation.

Fear.

Power.

He wants control of Dante's empire and the Ricci family. But he'll never get it. He tried to tear us apart, destroy our family from the inside, starting with Paige.

Well, he failed.

I unlock the metal door of the prison cellar and help Paige to her feet.

"Where are you taking me?" she asks. Her voice quivers, and as I help her up the stairs, she's shivering.

Is she afraid of me?

"Upstairs to shower and then to bed," I say. We still need to talk. There's a lot to be said but not here, not in the prison cellar with her caged like an animal.

I want to apologize, but I can't.

She took Nova.

Paige worked for Vance, and while she may have had good intentions, I'm still reeling inside from her actions.

43

PAIGE

While I take a hot shower, Moreno is situated on my bed, waiting for me to reemerge.

We have a lot to talk about, but all I feel is guilt weighing heavily on me. My intuition screamed at me that something was amiss at Nanny Agency, Inc..

I certainly never imagined that the reason was Vance and the fact he works for an opposing mafia family.

After I dry off in the shower and slip on a t-shirt and cotton shorts, I run a towel through my hair on my way back into the bedroom.

Moreno's shoes are off, his tie loosened.

He's spread out on my bed and looks sinfully hot.

"Have a seat," he whispers, his voice raspy and thick. He's trying to keep his voice down so he doesn't wake Nova in the next room.

She ought to be sound asleep by now.

He pats the bed and I sit beside him, leaving plenty of space between us.

Moreno doesn't seem pleased with that and grabs me by the hips, pulling me closer.

I don't expect his brashness, and his touch makes me giggle as I fall onto the bed.

He raises an eyebrow, staring down at me, his arm trapping me right beside him.

I inhale his scent. It's musky and mixed with smoke. He needs a shower as bad as I did, but I'm not about to point that out to him.

There's something hot about his power, proximity, the way he stares down at me. I press my lips together.

"You were saying?"

"Don't you ever lie to me again," Moreno says. He shifts on the mattress and grabs my wrists, pinning them into the bed. "Do you understand?"

I nod.

"I need to hear it, Paige."

"I understand," I say and lean up, wanting a taste of his lips. He should be forbidden, but I don't care. Everything inside me screams that he's here with me and hasn't tossed me out or had me murdered for my betrayal.

"Do you?" Moreno asks. "Those aren't light words to throw about. I need your loyalty, your honor, your commitment to the family and me."

I smile up at him. "Is this the speech you give to all your recruits?" I tease.

He snorts and leans down, capturing my lips hard with a searing hot kiss.

My insides sizzle and are warm as I wrap my legs around him.

I want him.

I've wanted him for longer than I care to admit.

I've been fighting the growing desire building inside me out of fear, but the thought of not being with him hurts more than anything I could ever imagine.

Is it too soon to be falling in love with him?

"Do you commit to the Ricci family and me?" Moreno asks. His forehead rests against mine.

"I'm loyal to you," I say. "That's all I've ever been," I confess.

Moreno's eyes shine with warmth. "Good." His breath falls to my neck, sucking the sensitive flesh. "Tell me you want me." His kisses are warm and make my insides tingle with delight.

I do want him.

I want more than just his kisses.

"Please," I whisper, my voice cracking.

It's difficult to speak as my thoughts get muddled. He's no longer pressing my wrists to the bed. His palm caresses my breast through my shirt as he brings his lips back to mine for another searing kiss.

He's teasing me with this slow dance.

I lift my hips, gyrating, needing more than just a simple kiss. "I want you to fuck me," I say, staring at him.

A wry smile flicks at the corners of his lips.

"Naughty language, Paige. I hope you don't talk like that around my daughter."

Moreno's eyes crinkle with mirth. He inches my shirt up and lets his lips linger, then caresses my bare skin before removing my shirt.

His eyes shine as he admires my breasts, lavishing each one with attention.

But I want more.

"You have too many clothes on." I tug at his shirt, ripping the buttons off in my attempt to open his dress shirt.

He stares down at me. "That's coming out of your stipend."

I think he's joking. I'm not entirely sure. "Then I demand a raise."

Moreno chuckles and pulls back long enough to remove his pants before I rip them open next. "Down, tiger," he says.

He does this to me, makes me wild with wanton need.

Never in my life, have I experienced sex like this, primal, instinctive, and blazing, intense like the heat of a thousand suns.

His hand is rough and warm, and he slips his digits inside my shorts. He rubs against my panties with two fingers, stroking my slit, teasing me.

"You're already wet for me," Moreno whispers into my ear.

He slaps my sex, and I no longer keep my moans silent and muffled.

Moreno shoves his mouth over mine to keep me quiet. His tongue pushes past my lips, and he pushes my shorts and panties down in one swoop.

He slides down my torso, his tongue flicking at my tiny bead, two fingers thrusting in and out of my sex.

My fingers bunch into fists, tangling in the bedsheets as warmth and wetness build inside me.

The room is several degrees warmer, and I feel the building crescendo of an impending orgasm.

My toes curl, and my back arches off the mattress.

He doesn't stop. His tongue keeps working its magic, moving at the same steady speed, driving me wild.

Moreno knows just what to do, and I'm tinkering over the edge before falling into oblivion.

As I gasp for air, my heart pounds against my chest.

My sex throbs for more from him.

One orgasm wasn't enough. I crave another. I want him.

"I'll be right back," he whispers, climbing off the bed.

I whimper in protest and sit up, watching his naked ass scamper into the bathroom. He opens the bottom cabinet and digs through a bunch of stuff that I've managed to keep cleaned up and hidden away.

"You'd better not have used my condoms without me," Moreno says.

"With whom?" I laugh at his absurdity. It's not like I'm sneaking men into my bedroom.

I haven't touched a man in months, long before coming to Breckenridge.

"Not who. What. You have a vibrator." He grabs the base and shows me from beneath the sink that he discovered my toy. Like I don't know that I hid it down beneath the sink in the cabinet.

I didn't think he'd go searching through my belongings.

"Kill me now," I mutter under my breath.

It's not like I can lie and say that it doesn't belong to me.

"This thing is getting tossed. I'm not having a toy satisfy my woman."

His woman? I bite down on my bottom lip to keep from grinning.

"Then you'd better get back over here and finish what you started," I say. "Or I might have to finish myself."

"Oh hell, no." There are a few more seconds of him rummaging under the sink in the cabinet. "Found it!" He grabs a condom and brings it back out to the bedroom, opening the packet and tossing the foil wrapper on the nightstand.

About damn time.

He unwraps the condom, and within a matter of seconds, he's pouncing on me, straddling me on the bed, his lips descending onto mine.

I reach down between us, needing to feel him inside me. My body is humming with excitement.

A moan escapes my lips as he enters me. While he buries deeper, I wrap my legs around him and toss my head back.

Each thrust is slow and drawn out, as we are building a rhythm together.

I run my fingers over his chest and then along his back, down to his ass, pulling him tighter.

He's taking his time, savoring every moment.

His lips cover mine, and I clench down, feeling the impending orgasm surface.

Moreno growls as he nips my lips, and his mouth moves to my neck, sucking the skin.

Each thrust is deeper, harder, faster as I pull him tighter against me.

My heart slams against my chest, and my eyes squeeze shut, back arching as he drives me over the edge.

He grunts into my ear, letting go, collapsing against my body.

I don't want to unwrap myself from him, but he untangles and retreats to the bathroom to dispose of the condom.

Climbing under the covers, I reach for the light, shutting it off beside the bed.

Moreno shuts off the bathroom light and slips under the covers with me, pulling me against him. "Sleep, Paige," he says, kissing me softly.

I want to remind him that his daughter is likely to see us together in the morning, naked. That we both should put something on since the adjoining door doesn't lock, but I'm too tired and hope that we're awake before Nova sneaks into my bedroom.

EPILOGUE
SIXTEEN MONTHS LATER
MORENO

The bastard, Vance, had it coming, and he ought to get exactly everything that he deserves.

The justice system should lock his ass up and throw away the key.

He thought that he could manipulate me? Paige?

Hell, no.

Vance is in for a rude awakening.

He is arrested on multiple charges, including kidnapping, assault, human trafficking, money laundering, murder, the list goes on.

The girls we rescued in an attempt to free Paige agreed to testify against Vance.

And after learning about his arrest, Paige and I speak with the local Breckenridge Police Department regarding Nanny Agency, Inc..

We both have suspicions that the business is a cover.

Well, I have suspicions that's how he is actively recruiting young women into his human trafficking operation.

Paige thinks the whole place is a front for laundering money.

She isn't wrong, either.

While I don't have any direct proof, we speak with the local sheriff, and they are able to bring in a young female FBI agent from out of town to go in undercover.

At the same time, the FBI also investigates Serene and Laura's murders further and are able to tie Vance to the murder weapon.

All in all, there is enough evidence gathered to bring down Vance, Nanny Agency, Inc., along with his second in command, Rafael, and one of his capos, Marco.

At least Paige and I both get a little closure.

And thankfully, while Paige had reservations about an inside man, we've seen no evidence that anyone infiltrated our organization or the family.

Vance is a liar.

Always has been.

Always will be.

There's relief in knowing my men can be trusted.

Nova has grown so much, started kindergarten, and is even more chatty than she used to be before her mother's death.

She's made half a dozen new friends, and while I'm cautiously letting them come over to play, I appreciate that she's a little social butterfly at school.

I'm sure I'll have my hands busy as she gets older, especially with the boys. I do not look forward to her dating.

Paige keeps reminding me that it's years away, but I can't help but worry about the type of troublesome young men she'll attract.

I look at myself in the mirror and know that I want better for my daughter.

She's not to date anyone in the mafia.

Ever.

My relationship with Paige has blossomed over the past sixteen months.

I trust her implicitly with my daughter and my heart.

Dare I say I love her.

And I want to marry her.

Make her mine.

Forever.

I intend to claim her, worship her, and make her part of the Ricci family.

Paige has moved from her adjoining bedroom with Nova into my room, which was my suggestion within the first month of us dating, so that we wouldn't have to rush to put on clothes and worry about a little intruder discovering our little secret.

Which isn't much of a secret.

Nova knows.

She snuck in the first night we slept together and climbed onto the bed to wake us up by jumping on the mattress. Thankfully, we were buried under the sheets.

Dante knows.

He heard us through the walls the first night we moved into my bedroom together.

We weren't exactly quiet.

Nikki knows.

I'm not sure how or when she figured it out, but I knew our secret was out as soon as Dante mentioned it to me.

All the guards know that Paige is mine, and if they so much as look at her the wrong way, they'll have to answer to me.

Protective much?

Yes, but it comes with the territory of being second in command. I must be ready if something ever happens to Dante, and if it does and he dies, I swear I'll bring him back just to kill him myself.

That's how much I want to be don.

Thankfully, our business is cranking along just fine with Vance out of the picture.

We still have to be cautious with the FBI in our backyard investigating the DeLucas.

Vance is currently awaiting trial. I suspect he'll be dead long before the verdict is read. Cowards like him who prey on innocent women and children don't survive long in prison.

Men like me end their life.

Lucky for him, I'm on the outside. Though, that doesn't mean I don't know a few men in lockup behind bars, willing to do me a favor.

They owe me.

And I intend on collecting.

————

Thank you for reading Captive Vow. Continue the adventure with Savage Vow.

I'm ordered to execute her...

I never expected to see her again.

We shared one wild night several years ago.

She had no idea that I work for the mafia.

I'm a savage, ruthless killer, but she's innocent.

She saves lives.

I take them.

She's a pediatric oncology nurse.

Could she be any more of a saint?

She entered the wrong hotel room.

There can't be any witnesses.

My boss wants her dead.

Her life is in my hands.

I intend to make her my wife to protect her.

She'll hate me but at least I can keep her safe.

·   ·   ·

This secret mafia baby romance features an arranged marriage and is the third book in the Mafia Marriages series. This book can be read as a standalone and ends with a happily ever after.

One-click Savage Vow now!

Ready for your next one-click read? Binge the Eagle Tactical Series starting with Expose: Jaxson or grab the boxset Eagle Tactical Collection.

And sign up for my newsletter to find out about new books, giveaways, and freebies: www.authorwillowfox.com/subscribe

I appreciate your help in spreading the word, including telling a friend. Reviews help readers find books! Please leave a review on your favorite book site.

GIVEAWAYS, FREE BOOKS, AND MORE GOODIES

I hope you enjoyed CAPTIVE VOW and loved Moreno and Paige's story.

Sign up for my Willow Fox newsletter

If you enjoyed CAPTIVE VOW, please take a moment to leave a review. Reviews helps other readers discover my books.

Not sure what to write? That's okay. It doesn't have to be long. You can share how you discovered my book; was it a recommendation by a friend or a book club? Let readers know who your favorite character is or what you'd like to see happen next.

Thank you for reading! I hope you'll consider joining my mailing list for free books, promotions, giveaways, and new release news.

ABOUT THE AUTHOR

Willow Fox has loved writing since she was in high school (many ages ago). Her small town romances are reflective of living in a small town in rural America.

Whether she's writing romance or sitting outside by the bonfire reading a good book, Willow loves the magic of the written word.

She dreams of being swept off her feet and hopes to do that to her readers!

Visit her website at:

https://authorwillowfox.com

ALSO BY WILLOW FOX

Dangerous Boss

Bossy Single Dad Series

Billionaire Grump

Mountain Grump

Bachelor Grump

Faking it with the Billionaire

Looking for kinkier books? Try these spicy stories written under the name Allison West.

Boxsets

Academy of Littles

Western Daddies Collection

Obey Daddy Collection

The Alpha Collection

Western Daddies

Her Billionaire Daddy

Her Cowboy Daddy

Her Outlaw Daddy

Her Forbidden Daddy

Standalone Romances

The Victorian Shift

Jailed Little Jade

Prefer a sweeter romance with action and adventure?
Check out these titles under the name Ruth Silver.

Aberrant Series

Love Forbidden

Secrets Forbidden

Magic Forbidden

Escape Forbidden

Refuge Forbidden

Boxsets

Gem Apocalypse

Nightblood

Royal Reaper

Royal Deception

Standalones

Stolen Art

Made in United States
North Haven, CT
25 August 2023

40737281R00232